They'd been dancing around this moment all weekend; both of them afraid of what would happen if they let their guard down.

She was tired of being afraid. She wanted him. Wanted him in a way that went far beyond sex.

"I've got all I need right here."

In case he didn't believe her, she forced his gaze to meet hers. Every muscle in his body was tense, shaking from restraint. In the shadowed blue light, she saw the desire struggling to break free. "Right here," she repeated, and brushed a kiss against his lips.

A groan tore out of his throat and he wrapped an arm around her waist. Chloe found herself yanked tight against his body. "Do you have any idea how difficult you are to resist?" he growled.

The roughness in his voice turned her insides raw. "Show me," she challenged, her rasp matching his.

He did.

Dear Reader

This book is about mistakes. Making them, correcting them and learning from them. It's a subject near and dear to me because, goodness knows, I make *a lot* of mistakes!

In Chloe Abrams's case, she's so busy running from the mistakes of her parents that she can't see that she's repeating history. Meanwhile Ian Black desperately wants to atone for his past mistakes—to the point of obsession. Neither of them believes they deserve a happy-ever-after. Thus, when true love lands at their feet, they stubbornly refuse to acknowledge their feelings.

Fortunately for them Mother Nature decides to play matchmaker—by brewing up a spring ice storm.

Readers might remember Chloe from THE MAN BEHIND THE MASK. That book introduced Delilah, Chloe and Larissa—three best friends looking for love in the Big Apple. Of the three of them, Chloe was the most cynical about lifelong happiness, so naturally I had to write her story next!

Writing SWEPT AWAY BY THE TYCOON was a blast! Chloe and Ian's romance is a great reminder that, no matter how many times you screw up, life always offers a fresh chance at happiness. My only regret is that the Blue Bird Inn doesn't exist in real life. I'd love to get stranded there.

By the way, fans of THE MAN BEHIND THE MASK will love the peek at Delilah's and Simon's future as well.

Finally, SWEPT AWAY BY THE TYCOON is my tenth Mills & Boon® Romance title. It's been a wonderful journey so far. I'd love to hear what you think of this book—and the others. Please write me at Barbara@Barbarawallace.com   Feedback is not only welcome, it's appreciated.

Happy reading!

Barbara Wallace

PS Keep an eye out for the third book in this trilogy. Larissa, the most romantic of the trio, gets her chance at love soon!

SWEPT AWAY
BY THE TYCOON

BY
BARBARA WALLACE

MILLS
BOON

Published in Great Britain 2014
by Mills & Boon, an imprint of Harlequin (UK) Limited,
Eton House, 18-24 Paradise Road, Richmond, Surrey, TW9 1SR

© 2014 Barbara Wallace

ISBN: 978 0 263 24229 4

Harlequin (
renewable
sustainable
to the legal

Printed and
by CPI Ant

n

Barbara Wallace is a lifelong romantic and daydreamer, so it's not surprising that at the age of eight she decided to become a writer. However, it wasn't until a co-worker handed her a romance novel that she knew where her stories belonged. For years she limited her dreams to nights, weekends and commuter train trips, while working as a communications specialist, PR freelancer and full-time mom. At the urging of her family she finally chucked the day job and pursued writing full-time—and she couldn't be happier.

Barbara lives in Massachusetts with her husband, their teenage son and two very spoiled, self-centred cats (as if there could be any other kind). Readers can visit her at www.barbarawallace.com and find her on Facebook. She'd love to hear from you.

Recent books by Barbara Wallace:

THE MAN BEHIND THE MASK
THE COURAGE TO SAY YES
THE BILLIONAIRE'S FAIR LADY
MR RIGHT, NEXT DOOR!
DARING TO DATE THE BOSS
THE HEART OF A HERO
BEAUTY AND THE BROODING BOSS
THE CINDERELLA BRIDE
MAGIC UNDER THE MISTLETOE

This and other titles by Barbara Wallace available in eBook format from www.millsandboon.co.uk

To Kumkum Malik.
Without your help and advice I would never
have started my publishing journey.
Thank you.

CHAPTER ONE

PLEASE SAY SHE was not watching her boyfriend hit on another customer.

Okay, perhaps *boyfriend* was too strong a word. After all, she and Aiden had never said they were exclusive. Still, Chloe Abrams figured they were, at the very least, serious enough that he wouldn't pass his number to other women *while she was standing six feet away*!

Wasn't as though he couldn't see her. Last time Chloe checked, between her height, her heels and her hair, she stood above the crowd by a good couple inches. Yet there he was, flashing his heavy-lidded smile at some blonde on the other side of the coffee bar, and Chloe would bet it wasn't because the woman had asked for an extra shot of syrup.

From behind her, she heard a chuckle. "I wondered when you'd catch on."

Great. As if the moment wasn't humiliating enough, the resident slacker decided to chime in.

"You know she's not the first one, right? Dude gives out his number more than directory assistance."

Chloe dug her nails into the strap of her designer handbag and pretended not to listen. A difficult task, since the slacker's voice had a silk-over-sandpaper quality that made him hard to ignore.

"Funny, he always gives out his number. He never asks the women for theirs. I can't figure out if it's because he thinks his company is that desirable or if it's because by having them call him, he gets off the hook for paying. You wouldn't want to weigh in, would you, Curlilocks?"

The strap on her bag crumpled, Chloe was squeezing so tightly. Problem with narrow city coffee shops was that it was hard to escape the crowd. In this case, the owner had crammed tables along the brightly colored walls, which meant that during the morning rush the patrons in line stood on top of those sitting down.

The slacker had first appeared shortly after the new year. If she was being honest, *slacker* wasn't the right word, but she couldn't come up with anything better. Every time Chloe came in—which was obscenely often—she would see him nursing a cup of coffee. A permanent ginger-haired fixture. Sometimes he read. Other times, she'd spy him bent over a pile of paper, scribbling away. Rugged, unshaven, bundled in a worn leather jacket, his no-nonsense presence jarred with Café Mondu's trendy atmosphere. Usually he kept to himself.

Until today, anyway.

"If you ask me," he continued in his quiet growl, "a woman like you could do a lot better."

Not really, Chloe thought, but she didn't feel like arguing the point.

"Your iced coffee is ready." In an obvious show of female solidarity, the other barista called out Chloe's order in an overly loud voice. First the slacker, now Aiden's coworkers. Was there anyone who hadn't noticed her humiliation?

"Thanks," she replied. If the slacker wanted to assume the acknowledgment was for his comment, too, let him. Stepping toward the counter, she loosened her grip on her strap, the motion causing the leather satchel to slide downward slightly and brush the blonde's hip. The woman stopped flirting long enough to glance over her shoulder. *That* got Aiden's attention. He immediately looked in Chloe's direction.

And winked.

Winked! Un-freaking-believable. He could have at least looked embarrassed over getting caught. No, the jerk winked, as if she was in on the joke.

"You okay, Curlilocks?" the slacker asked.

Okay? Try furious. Discovering Prince Charming was a jerk, she could handle. She was used to jerks. But to have him make a fool of her in front of the slacker and everyone else in the place? No way.

"Excuse me," she said, tapping the blonde on the shoulder, "but you're going to want stand back."

"Why?" the woman asked.

"Because of this." She raised her drink over Aiden's head and poured.

"What the—?" Coffee and ice streamed down the sides of the barista's face, plastering his shiny black mane to his cheeks. He looked like a long-haired dog after a bath.

Satisfaction gave a way better jolt than caffeine. "He's all yours, sweetie," Chloe said, tossing a smile to the blonde. "I've got better things to do." Turning on her heels, she marched to the front door.

The slacker rewarded her with a slow clap as she passed. "Well played, Curlilocks. Very well played."

At least someone enjoyed the performance.

"You did not." Larissa Boyd stared at her with wide-eyed admiration. "The entire iced coffee?"

"All twenty ounces," Chloe replied. "I've got to tell

you, those bangs don't look nearly as sexy when dripping wet." She sat back in her office chair, smiling with a boldness she didn't truly feel.

"What did he do?"

"Nothing. He and his new friend were too stunned to speak. I think everyone in the shop was." Except, that is, for the slacker. She could still hear his applause.

"Too stunned to speak about what?" Delilah St. Germain's ponytailed head poked around the cubicle wall. "I got your text. What happened?"

"Chloe caught Aiden passing his number to another woman, and dumped an iced coffee on his head."

Delilah's eyes widened to match Larissa's. "You did not."

"Is there an echo in here? Yes, I did. Blame temporary insanity."

"No, insane was when you started dating the jerk. This, on the other hand... I'm impressed. You've got guts."

Guts or really poor judgment? Chloe's rebellious high had started to fade in favor of foolishness.

Based on her friends' awestruck expressions, they disagreed, so she kept up the facade. She was good at that: pretending to be unaffected. "I prefer to say I struck a blow on behalf of misled females everywhere."

"Use whatever term you want. If I had been in your shoes, I wouldn't have had the nerve."

"Me, neither," Larissa said.

They needn't worry; neither of them would ever be in her shoes, and that wasn't simply because they were both engaged to be married. To begin with, her friends attracted a different kind of man. Nice men who believed in calling women back. Neither of them would be impulsive enough to dump a cup of coffee over a guy's head, because neither of them would be involved with a man jerk-offish enough to warrant the behavior.

Not that Chloe resented her friends' happiness. On the contrary. She couldn't be more happy. From the moment the three of them met at CMT Advertising's new employee orientation, Chloe had recognized her two best friends were different than her. They were soft and lovable, with a smiling optimism she couldn't muster if she tried. The two of them deserved all the happiness in the world.

"When you think about it, Aiden's the one with the nerve." Larissa's voice dragged her back to the present. "Giving his number out when you were standing right there? What kind of guy does that?"

The kind of guy Chloe dated. "Apparently it wasn't the first time, either. The slacker told me he's a regular directory assistance."

"Wait, who?" Delilah asked. She had a habit of tucking her hair behind her ear, a motion that caused her sinfully large diamond to sparkle as it caught the fluorescent lighting.

"The slacker. You've seen him. He sits at the front table every day." She was met with blank looks. "Leather jacket? Buzz cut?" How could they not have noticed him? "No matter. He's the one who told me Aiden writes his number on a lot of coffee cups."

"You believed him?"

Oddly enough, yes. "No reason for him to lie."

Delilah ran a hand around her ear again. "All the better you dumped his sorry behind, then. We never did think he was good enough for you."

"Delilah's right. Any guy who doesn't appreciate you is a jerk. You can do better."

"The slacker said the same thing," Chloe muttered.

"The slacker has good taste," Delilah stated.

She smiled. Naturally, her friends would rush to her defense, same as they did whenever her latest relationship went belly-up. Only Chloe knew the truth. That the betrayal wasn't all Aiden's fault. How could it be when she was the one genetically programmed to pursue doomed relationships? Short-term Chloe, good for a few laughs, but not worth sticking around for. Good thing she didn't expect more, or she'd have serious depression issues.

"Jerk or not, he was also my date for your wedding, Del." The brunette's wedding was two weeks away. She was marrying the head of their advertising agency in a black tie ceremony that would be filled with colleagues and society people. All of whom would have plus ones now, except for Chloe. She sighed. "Damn, but he would have looked good in a tuxedo."

"A tuxedo you were paying for," Larissa pointed out, placing a comforting hand on her shoulder. "Don't worry; we'll find you a proper date. One who can afford to pay his own way. I'm sure Tom has a friend."

"Or Simon…"

"Absolutely not." She'd rather go solo than take a blind date. Scrambling to find some stranger to take simply so she had a dance partner? Thanks, but she didn't need another short-term deal right now. "In fact," she said, thinking aloud, "not having a date is a good thing. Now I don't have to worry about entertaining anybody, and can focus on being the maid of honor. What if you have a bridal emergency? I'm supposed to be at your beck and call for anything you need."

"You're not funny," Larissa said, narrowing her eyes. "Beck and call" had been an inside joke for months. Ever since Larissa got engaged and turned planning her wedding into her life's work.

"Actually," Chloe replied with a grin, "I am very funny."

"Wait till you start planning your own wedding. You're going to want my help, and I'm not going to give you any."

"Oh come on, La-roo, you and I both know I plan on being one of those inappropriate cougars who dates your son's friends."

Larissa folded her arms across her chest. "You would, too, just to get me, wouldn't you?"

"You know it," Chloe said with a cheeky grin. When discussing her love life, she was very good at playing the irreverent, cavalier friend. Only after Delilah and Larissa returned to their desks did she let herself give in to the hollowness plaguing her chest.

She'd liked Aiden, dammit. So what if their relationship consisted mostly of meeting up at parties and clubs? Enough time had gone by that she'd started to think maybe he might be a guy who stuck around awhile. She should have known better. Sooner or later all men left. After all, a person had to be worth sticking around for.

"Well, well, well, look who's back. Should I grab my umbrella?"

The slacker's gravelly greeting seemed to inch its way up Chloe's spine, causing her to stiffen. Looking over at the front table, she saw him leaning back in his chair, a smile on his ginger-stubbled face. *You really need to find a better nickname,* she thought to herself. Smug Bastard might work today.

"I wouldn't want to waste a good coffee," she told him.

"Again," he replied.

"Excuse me?"

"You mean you wouldn't want to waste a good cup of

coffee again. Though now that I think about it, you didn't really waste yesterday's drink, did you?"

Chloe narrowed her eyes. She was so not in the mood.

"Not a morning person, are we, Curlilocks?"

"Depends on the company."

"Ouch." He clutched his chest. "You wound."

If only. She looked away, hoping he'd get the hint and stop talking. Being here was awkward enough without the commentary.

He didn't. "I've got to admit, I'm impressed. I wasn't sure you'd be back."

Neither was she, until she'd walked through the door. In fact, she'd stood on the corner for a good ten minutes, debating the decision, convinced the manager would toss her on the sidewalk the second she entered. Or worse, Aiden would throw an iced coffee in her face.

In the end, pride won out. Stopping for her morning iced latte had been part of her routine long before Aiden came into the picture. No way was she letting some two-timing coffee jerk change that.

"Why wouldn't I come back?" she asked Slacker. He didn't need to know about her indecision. "Like I said, they've got good coffee here."

"Better than good, if you ask me." To prove his point, he took a sip. Chloe noticed the side of his left hand already had ink smudges. Today was a note writing day, apparently.

"Although," he added, once he'd swallowed, "if I were you, I'd ask another barista to wait on me. In case."

"I'm not you," she reminded him.

He surprised her by raking his eyes up and down her entire length. "That you're not, Curlilocks," he said with a rough-sounding growl meant to make her insides take notice.

Chloe's hand flew to her abdomen. Something about the man's voice managed to get beneath her skin. He knew it, too; his eyes gleamed with cockiness.

Keeping her head high, she headed to the register, where Aiden waited. "Hey," she greeted.

"Good morning. May I take your order?"

That was it? Where was the glare? The terse words? *The recognition*? Surely she was worth some kind of reaction beyond a bland, generic greeting? "About yesterday..."

"Did you want a coffee?" The bland smile didn't slip. He was, for all intents and purposes, treating her like a complete stranger. As inconsequential as an out-of-state tourist. Punching her in the stomach would have hurt less. "The usual."

"Which is?"

The cut deepened. Chloe's eyes started to burn. She quickly blinked. He did not deserve the satisfaction.

"The lady drinks iced peppermint mocha latte."

Looking over her shoulder, she got a shrug from the slacker. "You know my order?"

"What can I say? Sit here long enough, you hear things."

"Don't you mean eavesdrop?"

His lips curled into a crooked smile. "Only on the interesting customers."

"No offense, but that's a little creepy." Even if her stomach did flutter at the idea that she qualified as interesting.

"You say creepy; I say observant. Sort of a potato-pot*ah*to kind of thing. I like people watching."

"Let me guess. You're a writer."

"If I am, then literature as we know it is in trouble," he said, punctuating the remark with a low chuckle.

How on earth did Del and La-roo not notice him sitting there every day? Even as possibly crazy slackers went, the man stood out in a crowd. What, at first glance, looked like street scruff was really very controlled. His hair was shortly cropped, and his not quite red, not quite blond stubble looked more like he simply couldn't be bothered with pulling out the razor than a lack of grooming. His battered jacket was similarly deceptive. Looking closer, she recognized what had been a very expensive piece of leather that had been worn till the thing molded to his broad shoulders. It reminded her of the basketball sneakers she couldn't give up even after she could afford better ones.

"See anything you like, Curlilocks?"

Crap. Chloe turned back to the register, hoping she didn't look too flustered. "I was admiring your jacket."

His chuckle was low and raspy. "This old thing? I've had her for years."

Her? Much as she knew she shouldn't, Chloe took the bait. "You gave your jacket a gender?"

"Sure. Why let the big ticket items have all the fun?"

"Interesting point," she conceded. "I supposed you named her, too."

"Don't be silly. That would be crazy."

As opposed to this whole conversation. Fortunately, Aiden chose that moment to return with her drink. "No need," he said, when Chloe reached for her wallet. "It's on the house."

"Seriously?" Didn't she feel like a heel now. Maybe she'd misjudged him *and* yesterday's situation. "That's really sweet of you."

"Don't thank me. I didn't do anything."

Her smile fell. "You mean you're not trying to apologize for yesterday?"

"Why should I apologize? I'm not the one who acted like a raving lunatic for no good reason."

No good reason? Chloe tightened her grip on the cup. He was lucky she didn't give him a repeat performance. "Who did then?" she asked, forcing herself to step back from the counter before she could give in to impulse.

The barista raised and lowered a shoulder. "Beats me. Note on the register says the next time you came in, your drink was free. Apparently someone appreciates acts of lunacy."

Chloe took another step back. The only people who knew what had happened were Larissa and Delilah, and as of last night, they'd vowed to boycott the café until "Aiden came to his senses."

"Must have been one of those random acts of kindness."

No, it couldn't be. A glance at the front table showed a definite sparkle in the slacker's ice-blue eyes.

"Why would someone pick me?" Particularly when she'd been rude to him? Regret stole at her insides.

Slacker leaned back, letting the hood of his sweatshirt become a gray cotton cowl around his neck. "Maybe that someone enjoyed seeing Don Juanista there get his come-uppance. I hear it took a couple hours to get the peppermint smell out of his luscious locks."

A snort escaped before she could stop herself. Aiden was so vain about his hair.

"Too bad I didn't snap a photo for the front bulletin board. I'm guessing there's an awful lot of women who wished they could have seen karma bite ole' Aiden in the rear."

"I'm guessing you're right." The realization brought back yesterday's humiliation in force.

Meanwhile, back at the register, Aiden had turned his

sights to another woman in line, his grease pencil seconds away from marking his digits at the base of her cup. "Doesn't look like karma bit all that hard," Chloe noted.

"Oh, but it will. You just wait. Ten years from now, that suffering musician look will have morphed into a receding hairline and a beer gut. Let's see how many women want him writing his number on their cup then."

Chloe swallowed another snort. "You paint an interesting picture."

"Interesting? Or Satisfying?"

"Maybe a little of both."

"Then my work here is finished." Slacker grinned broadly, revealing a row of bright perfect teeth. He had freckles, too, Chloe realized. The slightest dusting across the bridge of his nose, along with a couple of faint scar lines. Rugged, weather-hewn. He'd had a run-in with karma himself, hadn't he? Did he win or lose? Chloe wasn't sure why, but she had a feeling he would come out victorious in any battle.

A jostle from behind brought her back to reality. The gathering crowd meant eight-thirty was getting close. "I better get going," she told him.

"Already? The conversation was just getting interesting. Sure you can't stick around?"

"Unfortunately, some of us have to work for a living." As soon as the words left her mouth, she winced. Man buys her a cup of coffee and she insults him. *Insensitive, thy name is Chloe.*

"Just as well. I've got a meeting myself."

Chloe didn't call him on the obvious lie. "Do me a favor and if you see the 'stranger' who bought me the coffee, thank him, okay?"

"Sure thing. Enjoy drinking it—this time."

He winked.

Chloe squeezed her cup. Why'd he have to go and spoil a perfectly pleasant moment with a comment like that? Worse, why did her insides have to tap dance in response?

She'd retort, but the words didn't want to come out. Snapping her jaw shut, she marched to the door, barely avoiding a collision with a cashmere overcoat as she rushed past.

Ian Black watched her exit with amusement. Kid was trying so hard not to look flustered. She had swagger, that's for sure, although Ian had known that long before she'd tipped coffee over the Irish Casanova's head. The way she strutted in here every morning with her high heels and that long curly hair every morning, as if she owned the damn shop... Bet she walked into the Empire State Building the same way. You had to admire her display of confidence, whether it was real or strictly for show.

Her cacophony of curls blew back from her face as she slipped through the front door, treating him to a glimpse of her tawny-skinned profile, a golden flash amid the early spring gray. For a tall woman, she had surprisingly delicate features. Like a Thoroughbred horse, she was lean and leggy. A damn attractive girl, and the barista was an idiot for not treating her better. Ian had been watching the two of them flirt for weeks, disappointed when he'd heard Aiden say they were "hooking up." Ian had hoped the swagger meant she knew better. Thankfully, she'd come to her senses. Then again, let he who wasn't guilty of bad judgment cast the first stone. Sure wouldn't be him, that's for certain.

"One of these days, I'm going to insist on meeting somewhere less crowded," Jack Strauss grumbled as he unbuttoned his cashmere coat.

"Excuse me for frequenting my own business." Ian

nodded at the girl behind the register, who immediately moved to get Jack a coffee. "And you're late."

"Stop confusing me with one of your employees. Traffic was a bear."

"Driving wouldn't be such a problem if you lived in the city."

"Not everyone can afford the rent."

"Good grief, you're a laywer. Of course you can pay the rent."

"Okay, not everyone can afford your kind of rend. Did I say something funny?" he asked when Ian chuckled.

"Inside joke." He was wondering what Curlilocks would make of the conversation. She thought he was a bum. The color on her cheeks when she'd made the remark about working betrayed her. He would have corrected her if he didn't find her mistake so damn amusing. Ian wondered if, when she did find out, he should duck for cover. She looked as if she had quite an arm.

"Must be a good joke, whatever it is. I haven't seen you smile in a long time."

Draping his coat along the back of the chair, the silver-haired man sat down in the chair opposite Ian just as his coffee and pastry arrived. He took a large drink, then let out a breath.

"Feeling better?" Ian asked.

"Aren't I supposed to be asking you that question?"

Yes, he was. Much as Ian wanted to believe Jack's concern was as much out of friendship as it was obligation as his sponsor, he knew better. "Same as always. One day at a time.

"You're not…"

He shook his head. "No worries. These days I'm all about the coffee."

"So I see." Jack took another sip. "Although you didn't

have to go to such extremes. Most recovering addicts settle for buying cups of coffee, not coffee shops."

"I'm not most guys in recovery."

"No kidding. One of these days I expect to walk in
here to find you bought a coffee plantation so you can
grow your own beans."

"Don't think the thought hasn't crossed my mind."
Ian never did believe in doing things halfway. Military
service, business, alcohol abuse.

Hurting people.

Jack nodded at the stack of stationery by his elbow.
"Still writing letters, I see."

"Told you when we first started meeting, I had a long
list." He ran a hand across the stack. Twenty years of
being a rat bastard left a long tail. "Don't suppose you
have those addresses I wanted tracked down?"

"Again, stop confusing me with an employee."

"Are you planning to bill me for your law firm's time?"

When Jack's look said "of course," Ian stated, "Then
technically, you are an employee. Now, do you have the
names?"

"I'm beginning to see why your board of directors
ousted you. You're an impatient son of a gun." The lawyer reached for his briefcase. "My investigator is still
trying to locate a few people." He held up a hand before
Ian could comment. "You gave him a pretty long list."

"Could have been worse. Tell him to be glad I stuck
to Ian Black, the business years."

"Thank heaven for small favors. You do realize that
when the program says you need to make amends, you
don't need to literally contact every single person who
ever crossed your path."

You did if you wanted to do things right. "You make
amends your way, I'll make amends mine," Ian told him,

snatching the papers. He didn't have the heart to tell Jack the list didn't begin to scratch the surface.

Quickly, he ran his eyes down the top sheet. Three pages of ex-girlfriends, former friends, employees and associates, all deserving of apologies.

And one name that mattered most of all. He glanced up at his friend. "Is—"

"Last page. At the bottom."

Of course. Save the worst offense for last. Flipping pages until he got to the last one, he found the name immediately. His biggest mistake.

And the hardest of all to make amends for.

CHAPTER TWO

"WHAT DO YOU mean, don't call him?" Ian slapped his empty coffee cup on the table. Since they'd started meeting, Jack had done nothing but talk about the twelve steps. Make amends to the ones you hurt, ask forgiveness, etc., etc. Now here Ian was, doing exactly that, and the man was saying he shouldn't? What the hell?

"I didn't say you should never call him," Jack replied. "I'm simply suggesting you slow down. Amends aren't made overnight."

"They aren't made sitting around doing nothing, either."

"You aren't doing nothing. He answered your letters, didn't he?"

"Yeah," Ian replied, "but…" But letters could say only so much. It was too easy to censor what you were writing. Too hard to read what wasn't being said. In the end, everything sounded flat and phony.

"Some conversations should be face-to-face. I need him to hear my voice, so he knows I'm sincere."

"He will, but I think you still need to go slow. You can't push the kid if he's not ready."

"Who says he's not ready? It's not like I'm suddenly appearing in his life unannounced."

"Then why didn't he give you his phone number?"

"Because I didn't ask," Ian quickly replied. Truthfully, he should have called long before this. During those early months of sobriety, however, he'd been shaky—and all right, a little scared—so he'd let Jack and the counselors talk him into writing a letter instead. But he was stronger now, more himself, and he needed to face his son. "I'm tired of wasting time," he told Jack. "I've wasted enough."

Thirteen years, to be exact. Thirteen years during which his ex-wife, Jeanine, had no doubt filled his son's head with garbage. Even if a good chunk of what she said was true, it wouldn't surprise Ian if she went overboard to make him look as bad as possible. His ex-wife was nothing if not an expert at deflecting blame. Her influence made repairing his mistakes all the more difficult. He could already sense her lies' effect in the way Matt phrased his letters. So polite and superficial. Again, it was too easy to read between the lines. The only way he would loosen Jeanine's grasp was for them to talk face to face. "I'm not expecting us to plan a father-son camping trip, for crying out loud. I simply want to talk."

On the other side of the table, Jack shook his head. "Still think it's a bad idea."

"I didn't ask what you thought," Ian snapped. He already knew the older man's opinion, and disagreed with it. Jack didn't have children. He wasn't sitting here with the window of opportunity growing smaller and smaller. A year ago Matt was in high school; now he was in college. Three years from now he'd be out in the world on his own. Ian didn't have time to take things slow.

"Maybe not." The lawyer didn't so much as blink in response to the rude reply. Ian suspected that's why Jack had been assigned as his sponsor; he was one of the few people who didn't back down at the first sign of temper.

"But I'm giving it to you, anyway. I've seen too many men and women fall off the wagon because they tried to do too much too fast too soon."

"How many times do I have to remind you, I'm not your average addict." He was Ian Black. He believed in moving, doing. Too many people wasted time analyzing and conferring with consultants. Sooner or later you needed to pull the trigger. Getting to yes meant getting things done.

Which was why, as soon as Jack left for his office, Ian reached for his cell phone. The call went straight to voice mail. Hearing the voice on the other end, he had to choke back a lump. He'd heard it before, but never this close, never speaking directly to him. Hearing his son sound so grown-up... All the milestones he'd missed rushed at Ian. So many lost moments. He had to fight himself not to call back and listen to the message again. They'd speak soon enough.

Eleven hours later, though, his phone remained silent. He told himself to relax. Kid was probably in class or doing homework. For all he knew, they had lousy reception in the dorms and Matt hadn't even gotten his message. Ian came up with a dozen reasons.

None made him any less agitated.

Letting out a low groan, he scrubbed his hands over his face.

It didn't help that he spent the day writing letters of apology. A stack of envelopes sat by his elbow. One by one he'd addressed and ticked off names on the list Jack had supplied.

So many names, so many people who hated his guts and probably—rightfully—danced when they heard he'd been ousted from Ian Black Technologies. As he'd told

Curlilocks, nothing beat a healthy dose of karmic blow-back. *Curlilocks.* Aiden said her real name was Chloe, but he thought the nickname suited her better.

He probably shouldn't be thinking of her at all considering the shocking number of women he finished apologizing to. So many wronged women. Some, like his ex-wife, were women he never should have gone near in the first place. Others were opportunistic bed partners who'd hoped to become more. But many were simply good women who'd offered their affection and whom he'd let down. Their names stung the most to read. Business casualties he could rationalize as part of the industry; personal betrayals showed how toxic a person he could be.

Ian ran his finger across Matt's name and felt an emptiness well up inside him. The head roads he'd made in this relationship weren't nearly enough.

To hell with waiting. Patience was overrated. He grabbed his phone and dialed. Voice mail again. He slammed it down on the table, the force causing his empty coffee cup to rattle.

When he'd bought the coffee shop, the first thing he did was order new drinkware, replacing the cutesy china cups with sturdier, heavier stoneware. The kind that, when hurled, would leave their mark rather than shatter. What, he wondered, would happen if he tossed one right now? Would his employees duck in fear as they used to? The new and improved Ian Black vowed not to be a bully. But damn, did he want to heave something right now....

"Should I get out my umbrella?"

He looked up to find Curlilocks looming over his table. Even with his black mood, a rush of male admiration managed to pass through him. At some point during the day she'd corralled her curls into a high ponytail that controlled, but didn't completely tame them. She must have walked a few blocks because her nose and cheeks were bright pink from the harsh winter air that had taken up residence in the city that night.

"Little late for you to be roaming the streets, isn't it?" It wasn't like him not to notice her entrance. He wondered how long she'd been standing by his table. Long enough to witness his little meltdown?

"Working late. Came here for a refuel, because the office coffee stinks." For the first time, he noticed she was holding two coffee cups, one hot, one cold. She slid the hot one in his direction. "Here."

"What's this?"

"Call it a random act of kindness."

Ian stared at the white cardboard cup. Kindness didn't suit him at the moment. "No, thanks."

"Seriously, go ahead. I owe you for spending your money on me this morning."

Right, because she thought him down on his luck and was probably worried that he didn't have the money to waste. This morning he found her mistake amusing, but tonight it merely emphasized his current position, and the mistakes he'd spent the last eleven hours trying to amend. "I don't need your coffee. You want to feel charitable, try the guy on the corner." Someone who deserved the gesture.

Her eyes widened, their chocolate warmth replaced by humiliation. Ian immediately regretted his response. "Look, I just meant—"

"Forget it!" She held up her hand. "I was paying you back for this morning, is all. You don't want the coffee, then you give it to the guy on the corner."

"Chloe—" A blast of cold air killed the rest of his apology.

So much for the new and improved Ian Black. Why didn't he go kick a kitten, too, so he could really be a jackass?

Chloe strode from the shop as fast as she could. You try to do a guy a favor. Jeez, she'd bought him a cup of coffee. No need for him to make a federal case out of it. What did he think she wanted to do? Save him? Only reason she bought him the drink was because the café was about to close, and he'd looked a little lost staring at his empty mug. He didn't have to toss her good deed back in her face.

What had caused his sudden mood shift, anyway? The guy had been happy-go-lucky enough this morning. Did the day just wear him down? Lord knows sitting alone in a coffee shop all day would do that to her. Such a waste of what looked like a strong, capable man. More than capable, really.

Not that she studied him all that closely.

The wind bit her cheeks, reminding her that, at the moment, she was the one braving the cold, not her slacker. She flipped up the collar on her coat. It wasn't much protection against the wind, but at least she could bury her chin a little. With her eyes focused on the sidewalk, she dodged the sea of homebound commuters, wishing she could be one of them. Stupid slacker. It was his fault she was dodging anything. If she hadn't wasted half her day wondering about his story, she'd be on her way home, too, instead of heading back to the agency.

The attack came out of nowhere. One minute she was rushing down the sidewalk, the next her shoulder was being ripped backward. A pair of hands slammed into her back, hard, knocking the air from her lungs and her body off balance. Before she could so much as gasp she was pitching forward, face-first onto the sidewalk. Stars exploded behind her eyes as her hands and chin struck the cement.

From behind her, she heard a shout, followed by the scrambling of feet and a second, deeper cry of pain. A second later, she felt an arm around her waist.

"You all right, Curli? Damn, look at your chin."

"Wh-what?" Chloe was too dazed to answer. The arm around her waist felt warm and safe, so she leaned in closer.

"Your chin," her savior repeated, his voice soft and rough. "It's bleeding."

She touched her face, flinching when she felt sticky wetness. The dampness trailed down her scarf to the front of her coat. She tried to look down, to see the damage, but everything was dark.

"It's mostly coffee," he told her, but we should make sure your chin doesn't need stitches. Do you have anything in your bag I can use to wipe the skin clean?"

"I don't think—my bag!" She sat up a little straighter. That had been the tug she'd felt on her arm. The jerk had stolen her pocketbook.

"Right here." The soothing arm disappeared from her waist. A second later, a brown leather bag appeared in her lap, minus the strap. Chloe fingered the jagged end where the mugger cut the strap free. The bag had been her twenty-fifth birthday present to herself. Now it was ruined. Because some thug had got close enough to…

Her lower lip started to quiver. That made her teeth and chin hurt more.

"Shh, don't cry, Curlilocks. It'll be all right."

No, it wouldn't. "I—I was m-m-mugged." The word hurt to say. She felt dirty and violated.

"I know. I know." His whisper reached through the

cold, calming her. "If it's any consolation, they're hurt worse than you."

"They?" There were two? She started to feel nauseous. "I didn't see them."

"That's how it works. They find someone who's not paying attention and grab the bag from behind."

Fingers brushed the hair from her face. Tender fingers, but they made her tremble nonetheless. "You stopped them," she said.

"Right place, right time." The fingers found their way to her jaw. Tilted her face until she could see his pale blue eyes. Under the streetlight, his stubble looked more blond than red, the freckles across the bridge of his nose more prominent. "We really need to treat that cut," he said. "Do you have anything in your bag?"

Chloe shook her head. "Afraid not. I cleaned the thing out this morning." Thank goodness, too. Any heaver and the force of it being ripped away might have dislocated her shoulder.

"Lucky for you, I'm good at improvising." Before she could ask what he meant, he'd shed his jacket and begun peeling the sweatshirt over his head.

"What are you doing?"

"Relax. The shirt's fresh from the laundry." He mopped at the cut with one of the sleeves.

Chloe caught his wrist. "You're ruining your sweat-shirt."

"A sacrifice for a worthy cause," he replied.

By now, they'd attracted curiosity and several people had stopped to check on them.

"We'll be fine," the slacker told them. "Doesn't need stitches."

"How do you know?" She hated to admit it, but with

the gentle way he was dabbing at her wound, she wouldn't care one way or the other.

"Let's say I've seen my share of cuts and wounds. How are your hands?"

She turned them over. Road burn marred her palm. "I'm betting your knees match," he said. "Come on, I'll take you back to the coffee shop and clean you up properly. We can call the police from there, too. Chances are there's not much they can do at this point, but you should file a report, anyway—just in case."

Chloe could do little more than nod. The way her insides were shaking, she couldn't think straight if she tried.

Meanwhile, the slacker took charge, effortlessly. Letting someone else carry the load for a change felt good. When his arm returned to her waist, and he helped her to her feet, she couldn't help curling into his body. He smelled of coffee and wood. Strong, masculine, solid scents that filled her insides with a sense of security.

"I don't even know your name," she said, realizing that fact almost with surprise. "Slacker" definitely no longer applied.

He paused a moment before answering. "Ian Black."

Ian Black. The name sounded familiar, but she couldn't figure out why. Didn't matter; her rescuer finally had a name. "Thank you, Ian Black," she said, offering a grateful smile.

"You're welcome, Chloe." Hearing him use her proper name only made her smile wider.

They held each other's gazes, not saying a word. Finally, Ian stepped back, his arm slipping away from her waist. "What do you say we get you cleaned up?"

Right, her chin. Unbelievably, Chloe had forgotten.

"I'm not sure what I would have done if you hadn't

happened along when you did," she told him as they walked slowly back.

With the immediate drama over, adrenaline had kicked in, causing her legs to shake. She was afraid her knees would buckle beneath her if she moved too quickly. Ian kept pace a few inches from her elbow, not touching, but close enough to grab her should something happen. He held her bag tucked under his arm. The big leather satchel looked ridiculous, but he didn't seem to mind.

"I'm only sorry I didn't arrive a minute earlier. I might have spared your chin," he said.

Which throbbed. To make walking easier, Chloe had taken over the job of pressing it tight. She was pretty sure the bleeding had stopped long ago, but Ian insisted she maintain pressure. "I don't care about my chin." She'd suffered worse playing college ball. "I'm more bummed out about my bag."

"Pocketbooks can be replaced."

"Not at that price," she muttered.

"Then on behalf of your bag, I'm sorry I didn't move faster."

"You showed up. Better than nothing."

Why did he show up, though? He'd been sitting at his table when she'd left. She started to frown, only to have pain cut the expression short. "Were you following me?"

"Yes, I was."

"Oh." At least he scored points for honesty. She scooted an inch or two to the right. "Why?"

"To apologize," he told her. "I had no business being so rude to you earlier. You bought the coffee to be nice. I was wrong to bite your head off."

Had all that taken place tonight? The exchange seemed like eons ago. "Be pretty rude of me not to accept now, wouldn't it?"

"You wouldn't be the first person."

It was such a strange response, Chloe couldn't help frowning again. "What do you mean?"

She didn't get an answer. They'd rounded the corner to the coffee shop. A Closed sign hung in the window. "Shoot," Chloe muttered. "I'd hoped we'd get here before they locked up for the night."

"No worries."

There was a female barista wiping down the counter. Ian rapped on the window to draw her attention. Her chin must have looked pretty bad because the woman immediately stopped what she was doing and unlocked the door.

"Oh my God, what happened?"

Once again, Ian took charge, steering Chloe straight to the table in the corner. "We're going to need the first aid kit, Jesse."

Now, Chloe knew she had to be a mess, because the woman obeyed without a word. On the other hand, Ian's demeanor didn't exactly invite discussion.

While the barista disappeared into the back room, Ian made his way to the sink behind the coffee bar. Reaching into an upper cabinet, he retrieved a fresh towel. Then, grabbing a stainless steel bowl that was drying on the counter, he filled it with water.

"You look pale," he said when he returned. No surprise there. The shaking in her legs had spread to the rest of her body. Took all she had not to fall off the chair.

"Hold on." He crossed the room again, this time to help himself to a bottle of water from the display case. "Here. Drink some of this."

"Thank you." Drinking and keeping the sweatshirt pressed to her chin proved difficult, especially with her free hand trembling. Some of the water dribbled past her lips and onto the shirt.

"You're really making a mess tonight, aren't you Curli?"

Chloe was about to comment when she caught the twinkle in his eye. A smile tugged the corners of her mouth. "Good thing you didn't give me coffee. I might have stained your sweatshirt."

"Heaven forbid. Coffee's such a bitch to get out."

As opposed to blood. "I hope this wasn't your favorite shirt."

"A worthwhile sacrifice," he said again, then ran his index finger down the bridge of her nose before giving the tip a playful tap.

Fighting to keep to the color from flooding her cheeks, Chloe looked away. Maybe it was the change in temperature after being outside, but her chill had begun to fade, replaced by an odd fluttering deep in her muscles. Like shivers, only more intense and without the nervous edge.

"Here's the first aid kit. I can't vouch for the contents. Been awhile since we've had to use anything in it." Jesse's return removed some of the electrical charge from the moment. "I grabbed some plastic bags, too. In case you want to make an ice pack."

"Good idea. Could you make me a couple? You might want them for your knees," he added to Chloe.

As soon as he mentioned them, she lifted her skirt for a peek. Sure enough, both knees had quarter-size scrapes right below the kneecap. Dark red marred the outer skin, the beginnings of what would be large purple bruises. The cuts didn't hurt now, but they would soon. She looked around for a way to prop her legs so she could balance the ice bags. Finding none, she left her feet dangling. She'd ice the bruises later.

Meanwhile Ian was sorting through the first aid kit. "I see what you mean about the contents," he said tossing a half a roll of gauze on the table. "Better make an extra ice pack for her chin, too."

"Sure thing, boss."

Boss? The sweatshirt pressed against her chin was the only thing keeping Chloe's jaw from dropping. "You work here?" she asked Ian.

"Something like that."

"Define something." She'd caught the look Ian and the barista exchanged. Either he worked there or he didn't. Why the evasive answer?

Ian didn't reply. "We're going to be here awhile, Jess," he told the other woman. "Will you be all right getting home?"

"I'm meeting my boyfriend up the street for drinks."

"Be careful. We don't need a second incident."

Chloe waited until Jesse said goodnight before resuming her questioning "You could have told me you were an employee here." Might have saved her an afternoon of speculating if she'd known there was a perfectly logical reason for him to be hanging around. Not to mention saving her from being mugged.

"Could have, if I was an employee."

"But she called you boss."

"Uh-huh."

The answer hit her like a ton of bricks. Good Lord, but she could be dense, "You're the new owner."

"Guilty as charged. Ow! What was that for?"

She'd kicked him in the shin. If her knees didn't hurt, she'd kick him someplace else. "For making me think you were down on your luck," she snapped.

"I didn't make you think anything. You drew your conclusions all on your own."

"You still could have said something. Do you have any idea how much—" *Time I spent thinking about you*?

Thankfully, she caught herself before the rest of the sentence left her mouth. The hole she'd dug herself was deep enough, thank you. "Why didn't you correct me?"

"Let's say I found the misconception entertaining."

"Glad I could amuse you."

"Trust me, Curli, you did." His eyes met hers, their sparkle so bright and smug Chloe would have glared in return had her stomach not chosen that moment to do a somersault. She felt like an idiot. Her and her big grand gesture. "No wonder you told me to give the coffee to the man across the street."

"Figured he could use the warmth more than me." Moving closer, Ian lifted the sweatshirt from her chin. The fabric tugged the skin where the cloth had dried in place, causing her to wince. "Sorry," he said, tossing the garment aside.

"For the chin or for misleading me?"

"Both. Now, tip your head back so I can clean you up."

Although annoyed, Chloe did what she was told. A second later, Ian's fingertips brushed across her throat. She jumped, her frazzled nerves making the touch feel far more intimate than it was.

Ian sensed her discomfort. "Shhh." His thumbs stroked her pulse points. Again, intimate, but soothing. "I need to see how deep the cut goes."

As he spoke, he leaned in tight. Once again, Chloe found herself breathing in coffee and wood, strong, manly scents that calmed her nerves. His hands were softer than she expected. Given his gruff exterior, she would have guessed them to bear signs of exposure and hard labor. These fingers, however, had the surface of silk, with a touch to match. Hard to believe they belonged to the same strong hands she'd seen gripping a coffee mug this morning. Until he fanned his thumbs along the base of her throat, that is. Then she felt every ounce of their strength thrumming below. Controlled but ever present.

"You know," he said, his breath ghosting warm across her skin, "that was one of the reasons I ran after you. I wanted to set the record straight."

The sting of a wet cloth pressing against her cut kept her from responding. "Wasn't fair to keep stringing you along the way I was, especially after you made such a nice gesture."

"Nice, but irrelevant."

"Being irrelevant doesn't erase what you were trying to do." He rinsed out the towel and began dabbing at her chin again. "Good intentions should be acknowledged."

His answer brought back the odd fluttering sensation from earlier. She wanted to press her hand to her stomach, but their position made doing so impossible. Somehow, while cleaning her cut, he'd moved so close his knee had wedged itself between her legs. Or had her legs parted for his knee? She felt the seam of his jeans pressing against her flesh, making annoyance increasingly difficult to maintain.

"One," she said suddenly, grabbing the first distraction that came to mind. "You said setting the record straight was only one of the reasons you ran after me. What was the other?"

"I already told you, I wanted to apologize for being a jerk. I had no business biting your head off."

"Why did you?"

The only sound was that of water being wrung from the towel. "Long story."

And guessing from the sour way he spoke, not a very pleasant one. "Want to share?"

"Ever wish you could turn back time?"

Having expected him to say no, his question caught her off guard. "Beyond tonight?"

"Yeah," he replied, tossing the cloth into the bowl. Water splashed over the sides, leaving a puddle on the table. "Beyond tonight. Muggings don't count."

Then what did? Relationships? Bad decisions? "All the time," she answered. More than he could possibly know. She gave a soft laugh, trying to inject a little humor into what was otherwise a pathetic situation. "You met Aiden."

"True enough. What on earth did you see in him, anyway?"

"A really sexy Irish accent. What can I say?" she added, when Ian arched a brow. "I'm shallow."

"Aren't we all?" he replied with a smile.

Right now, the shallow part of her had noticed the shadows behind his eyes. The darkness alternately marred and enhanced their blue color, giving his gaze depth. "So why are you turning back time?" she asked him. "Don't tell me you have relationship issues."

"I've got issues up the ying yang, Curlilocks." His hands cradled her jaw again, tilting her head backward. "Let's see what we're dealing with."

"Will I live, Doc?" She really wanted to ask what he meant, but those were the words that came out.

Ian was quiet as he studied the wound. Amazingly, his touch was even more gentle than before. Between the featherlight contact and his breath blowing warm at the base of her throat, Chloe found herself fighting not to break out in a warm shiver.

"You already have a scar," he said after a moment.

"Took a header going in for a layup. College ball," she added for clarification.

"A six-foot-tall woman playing basketball. There's a stereotype."

"Six feet and a half inch, thank you very much." She lowered her chin, a mistake, since she found herself nose to nose with him. The shiver she'd been fighting broke free. "And playing ball helped pay for school."

"Lucky you."

"Suppose that's one way of looking at things." If you call being born with pterodactyl-length arms lucky. "I didn't really have a choice."

"We all have a choice," he said.

"What does that mean?"

Busy pawing his way through the bandages, Ian didn't answer right away. "Exactly the way it sounds. We always have a choice. We don't always make the right ones."

"You can say that again," she replied. "I've made enough bad decisions to qualify as an expert."

"Nonsense, you're just a baby. Talk to me when you've made as many mistakes as I have." He tore open a Band-Aid. "Then you can call yourself an expert."

Chloe recalled her thoughts this morning, about whether Ian had battled karma. Apparently he had, although not as victoriously as she'd supposed.

"All done," he announced, stepping back. He was referring to bandaging her cut, but intuition told her he meant the conversation, as well. The abrupt end left her as unsettled as his touch.

Made her wonder if she wasn't dancing around a mistake herself.

CHAPTER THREE

"Do you lie to everyone you meet, or did I win some special kind of prize?"

Engrossed in letter writing, Ian almost missed the question. He looked up to find Chloe towering over his table. She'd dressed for dramatic effect today, with her hair pulled back and a pair of large sunglasses accentuating both her cheekbones and her bandaged chin. Instantly, the memory of her skin beneath his fingers sent awareness rolling through him, and he had to squeeze his pen to keep from reaching out to touch her again. She was too attractive for her own good. The type of woman the old Ian would have pursued with a passion. Wined her, dined her and charmed those boots right off. On second thought, he'd charm off everything *but* the boots.

Damn the conscience that came with sobriety.

"Would you mind starting the conversation again?" he asked her. "I missed the beginning."

"Ian Black Technologies."

Ah. His not-so-secret identity. "Someone's been playing on the internet." He wondered how long it would take for her to dig up his story.

"Your name sounded familiar, so I went online to find out why, and there you were, larger than life. Ian Black, technology entrepreneur extraordinaire."

"*Extraordinaire*'s a pretty strong word. More like a guy who had the right idea at the right time. Still doesn't explain how I lied to you."

Her sunglasses rose and fell, signaling an arched eyebrow or two. "You said you owned a coffee shop."

"I do."

"Conveniently leaving out the part about the global defense company. A lie of omission is still a lie."

"Maybe I like keeping a low profile." The sunglasses moved again; an eye roll this time, he suspected. "Besides, I didn't omit anything. Or didn't you read the part where I got kicked out of my own company?"

"My ad agency works with a lot of large companies. CEOs get replaced all the time. Corporate politics, change in culture. Doesn't alter the fact you're hardly as down-and-out as you led me to believe."

Fascinating. She might the first woman he'd ever met who was annoyed because he was rich. She was also terribly naive if she thought his eviction was solely because of politics or culture change. "If you work in advertising, you know there's also such a thing as corporate spin. Believe me, I earned my ouster." Given how bad things got, he was lucky he'd held his office as long as he did. "As for the omission…I already apologized for misleading you. Defense contracting is part of my past. I prefer to focus on fixing my present."

"Fixing?" she asked.

"Told you, I made a lot of mistakes." He pointed with his chin at the two paper cups in her hand. "One of those mine?"

A blush made its way up those cheekbones, adding a shade of pink to the tawny color. "Apparently I didn't learn my lesson last night."

"Last night was sweet."

"Don't you mean naive?"

"Never apologize for doing something nice. So was buying coffee today." Regardless of whether he owned the place or not. "Besides, profits are always appreciated." He motioned for her to sit down.

"I wanted to do something to thank you for saving me," she said, settling into the place across from him. "I thought about buying you a new sweatshirt, but that was when I learned you were a big-time tycoon."

"Meaning I can buy my own."

"Meaning you could buy me one."

Ian laughed. She was a spunky one.

"From the looks of things, I'm going to assume you made it home okay, too."

"More than okay. I've never had a police escort before."

"I have," he told her. "Although they weren't as friendly." Nor did any of them check out his legs the way Officer Kent did hers.

"You didn't need to ask him."

Yes, he did. Curlilocks might put on a good show, but she wasn't as tough as she liked people to believe. Beneath all the spunk and saucy comments lurked a whole lot of vulnerability. If you looked close enough, you could see it flashing behind her eyes. Lord knows, he'd looked close enough last night. Exactly why he had asked the police officer to take her home. Talking, touching her.... he'd pushed his luck far enough. For a man who hadn't been with a woman in over a year, taking her home would have been way too tempting. He had enough mistakes to fix without throwing into the mix a one-night stand with a woman just out of a bad relationship.

"Don't sweat it," he said. "Part of the perks of being semi-famous is you feel okay asking the police for favors."

"No, I meant he'd already offered."

Oh. How considerate of the man. "Does this mean poor Aiden's been replaced?"

"No way," she replied with a wave of her gloved hand. "Not that Aiden's irreplaceable, because believe me, he isn't. I'm simply not looking to do any replacing. I wasn't kidding when I said I had a bad track record. I'm not what you'd call the best judge when it comes to people, as you know."

All the more reason he'd made the right decision last night. "How do you know Officer Kent wasn't the exception to your track record?"

Leaning forward, she lowered her sunglasses as if about to share a secret. "Because there is no exception."

"You sell yourself short."

"I'm not selling anything short," she said, wrapping her lips around her straw. "I know I'm a prize. It's the men that fail to meet expectations."

"Present company included?" Ian couldn't help himself; she'd left the door wide open. When she didn't answer right away, he laughed. "I'll take that as a yes."

"Seems to me a guy who lied about being poor shouldn't ask stupid questions."

Ian laughed again. No sense arguing, as she'd only reboot her lie-of-omission argument. Given neither of them were likely to concede ground, the argument would last all day.

They were alike in a lot of ways, weren't they? Stubborn, quick with the verbal cut. It's why he knew she wasn't as cavalier about men as she made out to be. The sunglasses might hide her eyes, but you couldn't kid a kidder. Last night's vulnerability tinged her voice.

Of course, she'd deny the charge to her dying day. Ian knew, because he'd do the same. Better to face the world with bravado. Hide the scars and fears, lest your weakness show.

So why did he talk about his mistakes last night? Reaching across the table, he pulled the other coffee close and peeled off the lid. The aroma of fresh brewed arabica greeted his nostrils. Hot, steaming and black. The one habit from his drinking days he never planned to drop. Closing his eyes, he inhaled deeply. *Heaven.* "What did man do before the invention of coffee?"

"Killed each other."

"In that case, I'm starting a petition to award the man who brewed the first cup the Nobel Peace Prize. I'm not sure, but I think his name might have been Starbuck."

This time Chloe was the one who laughed. Ruby-red lips parting to release an indulgent lilt. The sound wound through his insides, warming places long dormant.

He took a long drink, reveling in the relaxation. It had been a long time since he'd dropped his guard around someone—someone besides Jack and his rehab counselors, that is. No wonder he'd backed off last night. Subconsciously, he recognized the potential friendship and didn't want to screw things up.

"I should let you get to work," he said, setting his coffee down. "Going out on a limb, I'm going to guess you didn't show up early just to buy me a cup of coffee."

"If only. That is—" her eyes dropped to her cup "—I have to make up the work I didn't stay late and finish last night. I don't like leaving things hanging."

Me, either, he thought, glancing down at the letter he'd started and restarted a half dozen times. Another ex-lover whose feelings he'd crushed. Every apology he wrote was a reminder of how many "things" he still needed to address. "You have a good excuse, though," he told Chloe.

"I'm sure your boss will understand. Especially when he sees your chin."

"Why do you think I kept the bandage on?"

Damn, but he wished she wasn't wearing sunglasses. He liked the way her eyes sparkled when she got cheeky. "If you really want to ratchet up the sympathy, add a limp. Nothing tugs on an employer's heartstrings like a little hobble."

"Did the tactic work for your employees?"

"Hell no. Why do you think they were happy to see me go? I was a major hard-ass."

"So I read last night."

"And yet you still talk to me."

"Today, anyway." She started to leave, only to stop suddenly. When she spoke again, it was without the saucy edge. "In case I didn't make myself clear earlier, I really do appreciate everything you did last night. This probably sounds silly, but if there's anything I can do for you..."

"Don't sweat it. And you don't owe me a thing. Believe me, the good karma points are more than enough."

"Trying to avoid a receding hairline and beer gut?"

"You're onto me, Curli."

The corners of her mouth curled into a playful smirk. "I don't think you need to worry too much, *Ginger*. Man your age? The damage is already done."

Didn't he know it. Exactly why he forced himself not to watch her behind strut out the door. His blood was stirred up enough for one day. Stir it any further and he'd have to add another letter to the pile.

The transition from toasty coffee shop to the harsh outdoors hit hard. Chloe shivered and hugged her bag tight. She might have acted all laissez faire to Ian, but the truth was last night still had her feeling vulnerable. She

couldn't imagine how she'd feel if he hadn't been there
to lean on. His steady presence was the only thing keeping her from falling apart. If she concentrated, she could
still smell his scent. Twelve hours later, the memory alone
warmed her nerves. He'd been so strong, so dependable.
She wasn't used to dependable.

Of course, you could have knocked her over with a
feather when his photo popped up during her internet
search, and she found her slacker slash coffee shop owner
was none other than the CEO of a major defense company.

Former CEO, she corrected. A fact Ian had been quite
keen on emphasizing this morning. Something to do with
his abrasive management style leading to a power shake-
up. She'd been too shaky to do more than skim the story
last night.

Wonder where the ouster fell on his list of "issues"?
She'd ask, but feared opening a wound. Especially recall-
ing the pain he'd so clearly tried to mask when speaking.
And here she thought knowing the slacker's story would
end her speculating.

Up ahead, she spotted a familiar blonde head wrapped
in miles of dark blue scarf and moving slower than the
rest of the pedestrians. La-roo didn't do cold weather
well.

"Trying to dial the phone by telepathy?" she asked
when she caught up to her friend.

Larissa frowned at the cell phone in her hand. "I could
have sworn Tom said he would be in the office early this
morning. We're supposed to talk about groomsmen gifts.
Oh my God, what happened to your chin?"

"I got mugged last night." Chloe did her best to sound
casual, but her friend stopped short anyway.

"You're kidding! Are you okay?"

"Other than the chin and a few scrapes on my hands and knees, I'm fine. My bag suffered the brunt of the damage. Two hundred dollars down the drain."

"Thank goodness. You must have been terrified." Larissa took a step, then stopped short again. "What about your stuff! Are you going to have to cancel everything?"

"Fortunately, no. Ian tackled the guy before he could get too far, and saved my credit cards."

"Who's Ian?"

Chloe told her the whole story, including Ian's true identity, although she left out the part about last night's odd sense of closeness. Knowing La-roo, she'd get all romantic over what was nothing more than an overblown reaction to Ian's heroics.

When Chloe finished, her friend shook her head. "Unbelievable. This guy sits around a coffee shop all day? Why? I know running a small business takes a lot of time, but moving in seems extreme."

"No clue. Maybe he likes being idly rich." Which was doubtful. Ian didn't strike her as a man who liked being idly anything. He was more the man of action type. Like last night. She got a hot thrill just thinking about how he'd taken down the thug.

"Whatever the reason," Larissa said, "you're lucky he was there."

"Yeah, I was."

They pushed their way through the revolving door into the office building lobby. After three blocks of cold, the rush of warmth was almost tropical. Not as cozy feeling as at the café, but definitely welcome.

"I hate this weather," Larissa said, unwinding her miles of scarf. "I thought it was supposed to be spring."

"Early spring," Chloe reminded her. "You know as well as I do, that doesn't necessarily mean warm."

"No kidding. Did you hear they are predicting rain this weekend? If I don't see some sunshine soon, I'll go crazy."

"Cheer up. Another few weeks and you'll be in Mexico sipping champagne."

"The trip can't come soon enough. I only hope Del gets good weather for her wedding."

"Somehow, I don't think Del and Simon care, so long as they get married."

"True. Those two are so in love it's sickening."

Chloe had to agree. Both Delilah and their boss had worked late last night themselves. She wondered if they'd noticed she didn't return from her coffee run, or if they were too caught up with each other. Simon's door had been shut tight. She pressed a fist to her midsection. Inexplicably, thoughts of Simon and Delilah dissolved into an image of her and Ian, causing the fluttering sensation to return.

"You're one to talk. You've got Tom," she said, focusing her attention back where it belonged. Outward.

"I guess." Busy pressing the elevator button, Larissa sounded distracted. "Hey, is this Ian guy cute?"

Cute was the last word she'd use to describe Ian Black. "He's attractive. Why?"

She didn't have to answer; Chloe knew the reason as soon as she asked the question, and it was a bad one. "I'm not interested in getting involved right now."

"He's a step up from the men you usually date. A lot better than Aiden, that's for sure."

Was he? At least with Aiden, what you saw was what you got. Ian, on the other hand.... She barely knew the man and she already could tell he ran deeper and stiller than most waters. There was a reason she preferred shallow. Men with depth left bigger scars when the relationship ended. The nicks and cuts caused by guys like Aiden hurt bad enough. Why invite bigger pain?

"You know, there's no law that says people have to be in a relationship," Chloe said as soon as the doors closed. Thankfully, no one joined them, meaning they could finish this conversation in private.

"No one ever said there was."

"Then why do you keep pushing me to have one?"

"I'm not pushing anything. All I did was ask if this Ian person was good-looking. You're the one who went off."

Chloe looked at her shoes. Her friend was right. She had flown off the handle prematurely. "Sorry. Last night might have made me a bit oversensitive."

"Can't blame you there. If I'd been mugged, I'd be touchy, too. Although..." Larissa hesitated.

Glancing over, Chloe noticed her friend had literally bit her lip to keep from saying more. "Although what?" Might as well finish the whole discussion. When it came to certain subjects, Larissa could be relentless. Chloe's love life was frequently one of those subjects. "Spit it out."

"Fine," she said. "You're always so adamant about not wanting a serious relationship."

"I happen to like being single."

"So you say." Arms folded, lips drawn in a tight line, her friend was a five-foot-two-inch block of doubt. "I can't help wondering, who you're trying so hard to convince with your argument. Me? Or yourself?"

Under normal circumstances, Saturday morning meant sleeping in and drinking coffee in her pajamas. This Saturday, however, the bridal salon called to say her dress for Delilah's wedding was ready, so instead of being happily curled up under her comforter, Chloe found herself making the trek uptown. She wanted to run her errands before the rain started.

And she wanted to avoid Larissa. Chloe was still annoyed with her for that comment on the elevator. Who was she trying to convince, indeed. What a stupid question. Why would she need to convince herself of something she'd known for years? La-roo's problem was that she had an overdeveloped sense of romanticism. Her whole world consisted of brides, weddings and babies. Chloe was far more practical. She'd much rather preserve her self-esteem than chase some useless fantasy.

Thankfully, Larissa didn't notice how she'd dodged the original question: whether Ian was attractive. Big fat yes there. Even a dead woman would think so. For crying out loud, his voice alone qualified as sex on a stick. Add in the rugged features and obvious rock-solid torso, and who wouldn't be…intrigued?

Intrigued, though, didn't mean interested. If she happened to find herself walking three blocks out of her way to visit Café Mondu, it was only because she had a craving for a well-crafted iced peppermint mocha latte.

Just as it was surprise, not disappointment tightening her stomach when she discovered a pair of middle-aged women occupying the front corner table.

"Good morning," the barista at the counter said in greeting. It was Jesse, the woman from the other night. "Looks like Ian did a good job."

"Excuse me?"

"Your chin. The cut's healing nicely."

"Thanks." Chloe ran her fingertip along the scab. She still had a bump from smacking the sidewalk, but the redness had started to fade. "Lucky for me your boss has a knack for first aid."

"Must have been the army training," Jesse said.

"You knew about that?"

"I overheard him talking to a couple servicemen one day, why?"

"No reason." For a second Chloe worried that she was the only person in New York who didn't recognize the man. She'd learned online that his military service was an important part of the Ian Black corporate story. It was his experience as a medic that inspired him to invent the Black blood clotting patch that launched the company's success. "I only recently found out, is all. He's not here today, is he?" she added. Only because it would be rude not to say hello.

Jesse didn't have to answer, for at that moment Ian's stage whisper reached her ear. "For crying out loud, Jack, you make it sound like I'm popping in on the kid out of the blue. We've been in contact."

He walked through the storage room door, cell phone tucked under one ear, a coffee cup clutched in the other. Chloe nearly dropped her dress bag. Today was the first time she'd seen Ian without his vagabond clothes, and the result was breathtaking. He'd shed the sweatshirt and ratty jacket in favor of khakis and a sweater the same light blue as his eyes, making him look every inch the successful entrepreneur he was purported to be. He'd pushed the sleeves of his sweater to the elbows. Chloe tried hard not to stare at his exposed forearms. She'd never been one to care about arms and hands before, but Ian's were extraordinary. So hard and lean you could see the muscles playing with every move. A jagged scar ran down his right arm. It began beneath the cuff and traveled to his wrist. As Chloe followed the line with her eyes, she recalled how capable his hands were. Strong yet tender. The consummate male touch.

A flush washed over her. Why on earth did this man waste himself on baggy sweatshirts?

"Because some things can't be said long distance, and the longer I wait..." He pinched the bridge of his nose, clearly unhappy. "My gut says different."

"Three eighty-five," Jesse said. Chloe handed her a five dollar bill and waved off the change. She was far more interested in the conversation behind the counter.

"Fine. Your opposition is duly noted." Heaving a sigh loud enough to be heard across Manhattan, Ian slammed the phone onto the counter.

Chloe spoke without thinking. "Problem?"

He'd been staring at his cell and didn't hear her come around to his side of the counter. Her question caused him to look up suddenly, revealing a look of such weariness, it tore her insides in two. "Difference of opinion," he replied. He looked back down at the phone and sighed. "Damn. Now I'm going to have to call back and apologize at some point for hanging up."

"Sounded like this Jack person ticked you off pretty good."

"Nah, more like me taking my frustrations out on him. A habit I thought I had a handle on."

"Sorry," she replied.

Ian frowned. "What are you sorry about?"

To be honest, she wasn't quite sure. The lack of sparkle in his eye made her want to say something. "You being frustrated."

"No need to be sorry there. It's my own damn fault."

"Anything I can do?"

As expected, he shook his head. "If only, Curlilocks. Afraid this is a problem only I can fix. I just wish people would stop giving me advice I didn't ask for."

"I hear ya there," Chloe said, thinking of Larissa. "My

friends are very big on advice. I wish I could make them understand that when it comes to my life, I know best."

"Exactly." A fabric of understanding wove them together as he gave her the first smile of the day. A half smile, with a hint of sadness, but a smile nonetheless. "I keep trying to explain to him these are my mistakes. I need to fix them my way. Especially this one."

Must be one helluva mistake for him to react so strongly, but then, some events marked you more than others.

"I take it this Jack disagrees."

"To put things mildly. I swear, if he had his way, I'd still be on step one."

"Step one?"

"Yeah, out of twelve. I take it that that fact didn't show up during your internet search.

"What fact?"

He reached for the nearby coffeepot and poured himself a cup. "That I'm a drunk."

CHAPTER FOUR

"TECHNICALLY, FUNCTIONAL ALCOHOLIC would be a better term, since I preferred to keep a steady day-long buzz rather than get rip-roaring drunk. Enabled me to—"

"Function?" The remark came out far more sardonically than Chloe meant it to.

Ian saluted her with his cup. "Couldn't build a company otherwise."

Following his pronouncement, the two of them moved their conversation to a nearby table. In a way, Chloe was surprised he wanted to talk with her about such a personal subject. On the other hand, she wouldn't deny being curious. Not so much regarding his alcoholism as the shadow crossing his features. She'd seen the same shadow the other night. The slip suggested that while Ian spoke matter-of-factly, he felt far from casual about his past. His mistakes, whatever they were, struck him hard. If he wanted or needed a sympathetic ear, then she was willing to listen.

"What happened?" she asked him. A naive question, but she didn't know where else to start.

"I drank. A lot," Ian replied. "You mean how did the drinking get out of hand, though, don't you?" He shrugged and focused on stirring his coffee. "There wasn't any kind of traumatic event or anything. Started out with a few drinks to de-stress. As the stress grew, so did the drinks. Before I knew it, I was drinking all the time."

There was more to the story; Chloe could tell by the way he avoided her eyes. She was willing to bet that missing component caused the shadows, too. "What about work?"

"Functional, remember?" He laughed over the rim of his coffee. "Work was everything. Well, everything other than alcohol. The rest of the world took a backseat.

"People especially," he added in a soft voice. This time Chloe caught the shadows.

"Anyway, about eighteen months ago, I started the program, and I've been busy working on step eight—making amends to the many, many people I hurt."

Fixing his mistakes. Understanding clicked in, setting off a swell of admiration in her chest. She'd been right, he did beat karma. Leading her to the puzzling phone call she'd overheard a few minutes earlier. "Is your friend Jack one of those people you have to apologize to?"

Ian offered another mirthless laugh. "Jack's my sponsor. I deep-sixed my friends, good, bad and otherwise, a long time ago. In case you didn't guess by the fact I'm sitting here pouring out my guts to you."

So he did need someone to talk to. "I don't mind." If anything, she was flattered to make the cut. Meaningful conversation didn't happen with the men who usually crossed her path. Ian's inclusion made her feel substantial.

"You've only just met me. Give me time."

Meaning what? That he'd deep-six her, too? The comment made her nerves flare onto to quickly extinguish when she saw the melancholy in his eyes. Reminding her that his story was far from over. "I'm confused. Why doesn't your sponsor want you to make amends? Isn't he supposed to be encouraging you?"

"This is where we come to the unsolicited advice," Ian replied. "Jack thinks I'm moving too quickly. I need to 'move with caution' to use his favorite phrase. He doesn't get that I can't afford to move slowly. I've already wasted thirteen years."

A long time. Chloe watched Ian sip his coffee, trying to hide the expression she knew matched his voice. Her own drink had grown lukewarm long ago. She didn't care. His story was far too engrossing.

"This person must be pretty important to you, to want to reach out after a decade and a half," she noted. Or else the crime so egregious he couldn't forget.

"He is," Ian said. "He's my son."

His son. Her insides froze, killing the sympathy she had regarding Ian's pain.

"You abandoned your family?" She didn't bother hiding the edge in her voice. A man who abandoned his child didn't deserve consideration. To think she'd actually thought Ian was different. Better.

"Not entirely. I gave financial support. Paid his and Jeanine's—ex-wife's—bills. Made sure he lived well, but otherwise I kept my distance. Figured he was better off."

Oh yeah, the kid was so much better off. All those years, wondering what he'd done to chase his father away. Thinking he must be horrifically damaged if his own parents couldn't love him.

"You get what you deserve," she murmured.

Ian mistakenly thought she meant him. "You won't get an argument here. I wrote to him once I thought sobriety was going to stick. We've been corresponding for about a year now."

"Letters and money," Chloe repeated. More than she

ever got from her father. Still, the kid deserved better. Apologies were as flimsy as promises. More often than not the child still ended up with her nose pressed against the picture window, waiting in vain.

"Not enough, I know," Ian agreed. "I wish I had an excuse, but the truth is I was a miserable son of a bitch and a drunk. He *was* better off without me around."

"Do you honestly believe that?"

"I know it." He washed a hand over his face, leaving an expression of regret behind. "I was not a nice person, Chloe. I stepped on and hurt a lot of people to build my company. I would have hurt him, too."

"And a lifetime of being without a father didn't?"

"Hurt him a lot less." Ian sounded so resolute, Chloe decided not to argue. Perhaps he had a point. Drive-by visits certainly didn't do her any good other than trick her into hoping again.

Shaking off the memories, she returned to the topic at hand. "So what is it Jack doesn't think you should do?"

"I got Matt's number, and I called him. There are things that can't be said in a letter."

Yes, there were. "What did Matt say?"

"He hasn't returned my call yet. I told Jack I wanted to drive out to see Matt in person. That's where you walked in."

Ian's long fingers played with the cup handle, tracing the top curve again and again. Disappointed as she was, Chloe still watched the movement, remembering how those fingers had drifted across her skin. It hurt to think a man capable of such tenderness could hurt people.

"He thinks I should stick with letter writing," he continued. "But Matt's my son. He needs to hear the apology out loud. So he knows I'm serious."

A kernel of sympathy worked its way toward Chloe's

heart. It was clear Ian regretted his behavior. Pain clung to every word he spoke. And he was trying to repair the damage. Letters, a phone call. Driving to see the boy. What she wouldn't give for one of those efforts.

"I know I forfeited my rights as a parent a long time ago," he continued. Chloe couldn't tell if he was making his argument to her or himself. "All I want is five minutes so I can let Matt know I didn't forget him. My staying away was for his own good."

He reached into his wallet and handed her a photograph. "His high school graduation picture. I asked him to send me one."

Chloe saw a handsome boy with tight auburn curls and a wary smile. She could identify with the wariness. It was the fear that the camera would capture the inner flaws. "Handsome boy. Looks like his father."

"Smart, too. Salutatorian of his class. You should have heard the speech he gave at graduation."

"You were there?" In her surprise, Chloe nearly dropped the picture. "Why didn't you go see him then? Were you...?"

He shook his head. "Not at graduation."

"Then why not let him know?"

"I didn't want to ruin his day. His mother and I can't be in the same room without killing each other. I always made a point of flying under the radar so he wouldn't get caught in the middle."

Always? "You attended other events?"

"As many as I could. Just because I wasn't visible in his life didn't mean I didn't care."

A lump rose in Chloe's throat. Ian couldn't say more magical words if he tried. During how many basketball games, art shows and teacher nights had she fantasized about her father hiding in the back? Ian had done exactly that for his son.

How she envied Matthew Black. Ian was offering his son the gift of a lifetime—the chance to know he mattered.

She reached across the table and grabbed Ian's hand. "Jack's wrong. Your son deserves to hear your apology in person. Don't let him talk you out of going."

Ian stared at the fingers resting on his arm, soft and golden against his own pale skin. Comfort seeped from her touch, warming places inside him he hadn't realized were cold. Common sense said he should pull away, but his selfish side wanted to enjoy the sensation. "Sweetheart, did you read any of those internet articles? Once I make up my mind, you'd need an atomic bomb to move me from my position."

"So you're going to see your son."

He nodded. "Today. He's attending the state university in Pennsylvania." The trip couldn't be more than three or four hours. With luck, he could be there by late afternoon, and home before midnight.

Chloe was smiling. "Good. The sooner the better, if you ask me." She spoke emphatically, with an unreadable emotion behind her words that didn't fit the situation. From the glow in her eyes, you'd think she was the one receiving the apology.

"No offense, but for a woman who heard my story only five minutes ago, you sound pretty darn invested." Reluctantly removing his arm from her grip, he sat back so he could better see her face. "How come?"

"No reason." Her darkened cheekbones disagreed. "You're doing a good deed. I'm showing support."

"Good deed? Hardly." This apology was as much

for him as it was for Matt. Guilt over his many sins had driven him to drink in the first place. If he didn't atone for his mistakes—or at least make every effort he could—how long before the face he saw in the mirror drove him to drink again?

So no, his actions weren't good. Like everything he did, they were underscored by selfishness. The last thing he needed was a beautiful young woman looking at him with stars in her eyes.

Much like Chloe was looking at him right now. As though he was about to climb Mount Everest or cure cancer. A man could live on a look like that for days. If he deserved the admiration. "I'm no hero," he said. Reminding her and himself.

"At least you're reaching out to your son and letting him know you care. Some fathers couldn't care less."

Hers, perhaps? The way the sparkle faded from her eyes suggested as much. Ian's insides hurt at the thought. Then again, maybe it was his own guilty conscience needling him.

He could ask her, but the mood had already grown far too somber and serious. Funny how he opened up around her. Even after pulling back the other night, here he was, sharing his biggest secrets. It wasn't as though he couldn't stop himself, either. He simply felt comfortable around her in a way he never felt around anyone else.

Looking for a lighter topic, he spied the black garment bag draped over the spare chair. "Shopping?"

"Excuse me?" Chloe pulled her thoughts out of whatever fog they'd disappeared into.

"The dress bag."

She shook her head. "Maid of honor dress. My friend Delilah is getting married next week. To our boss, if you can believe it."

"That's one way to get a promotion."

"Aren't you cynical?"

Ian laughed. "Occupational hazard." For as many women whose hearts he'd broken, there was an equal number who'd been after the money.

"I didn't realize coffee vendors were such a catch," Chloe replied.

He laughed again. This was why he enjoyed talking with her. "Haven't you heard? Caffeine's the new sexy."

"Thanks for the tip."

"As for your friend...?"

"Delilah. In this case we're talking real, honest-to-God true love. If there is such a thing as soul mates, it's Simon and Delilah."

"Now who's sounding cynical?" There was a definite weariness in her last sentence.

"I'm not cynical. I'm broke. Both of my best friends are getting married this spring, and I'm maid of honor at both ceremonies. Although, on the plus side, I do get some completely useless dresses out of the deal."

There she went, acting cavalier again. Without the sunglasses to shade her eyes, the act didn't work as well. "You can always pay them back by getting them a completely useless wedding gift," he suggested. "Gold-plated salt and pepper shakers, pearl-handled shrimp forks. Just make sure you stay away from silver candlesticks. I still have the scar from when my ex-wife tossed one at my head."

Chloe winced. "Ouch."

"Ouch indeed." She didn't know the half of it. "In fairness to the candlesticks, the injury wasn't their fault. Jeanine and I were the equivalent of gasoline and a match. Some people aren't meant to have relationships."

"No, they are not."

Referring to himself, he didn't expect to hear her agree so quickly. Or with so much bite. "You're bitter because your boyfriend cheated on you." Which reminded him, he needed to stick Aiden on a few more late-night Saturday shifts.

Chloe reached for her coffee. "For your information, I am completely over Aiden," she told him.

"You sure?"

"Honestly? Other than the embarrassment factor, I wasn't all that into him."

Then what caused the shadows behind her smile? Something—or someone—had given rise to her jadedness. If not the Irish barista, then who?

Ian's thoughts returned to her earlier comments regarding parents. Fathers could screw up so much, he realized with sudden despair. What if Matt felt the same way about relationships? Jeanine had never married again. Ian...well, his dating history was well documented. Had he doomed his child to a life as cold and meaningless as his own?

"What's wrong?"

Ian shook his head. "Nothing. I was thinking I should get on the road soon, if I'm going to make it to the school before dark."

"I didn't realize the time," Chloe said, glancing down at a watchless wrist. "I'm sorry to keep you."

"Don't apologize. I'm glad you stopped by. It was nice having someone to listen." He stared at the hand resting on the table, his own itching to entwine their fingers. To physically connect as they had moments before. Needing a distraction, he grabbed his cup, hoping coffee replaced needs besides "Like I said, I don't have many friends anymore."

"You have at least one now."

She meant her. The declaration settled over his shoulders, solid and warm, like an invisible embrace. Friendship was a luxury he hadn't afforded himself in a long time.

"A very sweet one, too." How long before he let her down? If he listened to the ache pulsing through his limbs, it was only a matter of time before he turned a touch into another mistake.

No reason to make the mistake today, he decided, and stuffed his hands in his pockets. "Rain's getting heavier. I better grab a cup of coffee and hit the road. Next time you come in, the coffee's on me."

"Again?"

"Again," he repeated with a grin. "We're developing a pattern."

"Might be easier to buy our own and call it even."

"Might be."

He was dragging his feet. As soon as he left the coffee shop, he would be on his own, and while he normally didn't mind solitude—had grown used to it, even—he wasn't quite ready to leave Chloe's warm presence.

"Would you like some company?"

Focused on walking to the counter, Ian almost missed the question. When he finally realized what she'd said, he had to stop and repeat the question in his head, to make sure he heard correctly. "You want to come to Pennsylvania?"

"Why not? I don't have anything planned. Plus I could help distract you if you get nervous."

"I don't get nervous," he told her. "I get focused."

She shrugged. "Hey, if you don't want the company, just say so."

"I didn't say that."

"Then what are you saying?"

"I…" This wasn't a conversation he felt like having from opposite sides of the coffee shop. Making his way back to the table, he stopped short of her crossed legs. "Why?" he asked her.

"I don't understand."

Yes, she did; she was dodging the question. Ian leaned in. The fact that Chloe had stayed seated gave him a height advantage, and he had to admit he enjoyed the way her chin tilted upward. "Do you always offer to go away with men you barely know?"

She jutted her chin higher. "A day trip isn't exactly going away. Besides, barely knowing me didn't stop you from telling me your life story."

"Curlilocks, I haven't come close to telling you my life story." Nor, he realized, had she told him hers. Other than knowing she'd played college ball, worked in advertising and had lousy taste in boyfriends, he knew very little about Chloe Abrams. Hell, the only reason he knew her last name was because of Aiden.

"You still haven't answered my question. Why would you want to drive to Pennsylvania with me?"

"Because I owe you for the other night. You were there when I needed you. This is my chance to be there when you need someone."

"And?" he asked, digging.

"Does there have to be an 'and'? Isn't wanting to pay back your kindness enough?"

"Sure, for some people." Something, though made him think her offer wasn't totally out of obligation, even if she did sound sincere. After all, while he might not run a major corporation anymore, he was still a very wealthy man. An enterprising woman might easily think his recent spiral made him especially vulnerable.

"I'm simply trying to be a friend," she said, reading his mind.

"A friend, huh?"

"You don't believe me."

"I've been sold that line before."

"Trust me, it's not a line this time."

"Well, I could use a friend...." His eyes swept up the length of her. Along the mile-long legs, the squared-off shoulders, every inch a study in indifference. Until, this is, he reached her eyes. There, despite her best effort to hide it, he caught a flash of vulnerability. A little-girl-lost quality that could wrap a stranglehold around his insides if he let it. Any kind of relationship with this woman was a bad idea.

At the same time, they were talking about one day. Ten hours tops. It would be kind of nice, having an ally for once.

"All right," he said, his better judgment kicking him. "But I'll give you fair warning. I don't do pit stops or side trips, and I pick the radio station."

CHAPTER FIVE

"Last chance to change your mind," Ian said, placing Chloe's garment bag over the backseat of his SUV. "I can still drop you off at your apartment instead."

It was the third such offer he'd made, the first one coming as they were leaving the coffee shop, and the second issued in the parking garage elevator. "Are you trying to make me change my mind?" she asked.

"Just trying to be certain. Never let it be said I didn't give you the opportunity to back out."

"Or that you know how to accept a nice gesture."

"Been a while since anyone's made one, so I'm out of practice."

The comment made her sad. No friends, no kindness. Ian had painted a pretty lonely picture of his existence this morning. No wonder he'd turned to drinking. Unless the drinking had caused the isolation. Chloe suspected a little bit of both. One big, lonely circle. At least she had Larissa and Delilah in her life.

Speaking of which, both of them would completely overreact if they knew about this field trip. Delilah would sigh and make some comment about impulsiveness, while Larissa would, of course, bring up Chloe's comment about never having a relationship. Her friends wouldn't understand that her offer was neither impulsive nor one of her short-term flings. Her reasons were far more personal. A part of her needed to witness Ian's apology, to prove that fathers who deserved redemption existed, even if she never experienced the phenomenon herself.

"You think we'll be back by midnight?" she asked, sliding into the front seat.

"Why? Will you turn into a pumpkin if we don't?"

"You'll have to wait and see."

The grin he flashed her while shutting the door was nothing short of knee-buckling. "Lucky for you I like pumpkin."

The wiper blades made a soft swishing sound as they pulled out into traffic. At some point between their entering the garage and driving to the first level, the sky opened up, and the rain began falling heavier than ever. "Hope you weren't planning on a sunny Saturday drive," Ian said.

"I wasn't planning on a Saturday drive, period, remember?"

"True. You act on impulse a lot, don't you?"

She was pretty sure every inch of her skin blushed. "What gives you that idea?"

"No reason. You'll notice I brought extra napkins, though, in case your coffee accidentally flies out of your hand."

Pour one drink over one person's head... "I'm never going to live the other morning down, am I?"

"No way. Far as I'm concerned, the other morning will live in infamy," he told her. "Not that I'm one to judge anyone's bad behavior, given my history."

No, he wasn't. At the same time, Chloe had a nagging sensation that perhaps he judged himself too harshly. Granted, he'd made a killer mistake when it came to his son, but what other mistakes was he atoning for? Dammit, she wished she'd read those articles more closely.

She watched Ian navigate the New York traffic, noticing how the skin around his knuckles pulled taut as he squeezed the steering wheel. Who could blame him? This reunion meant a lot, and their current conversation led straight to his failing.

"What's he studying?" she asked, hoping the change in subject would distract Ian. "Your son. Do you know?"

There was no mistaking the pride in his voice. "Engineering. Got a full ride, too."

"Sounds like he got his father's head for technology."

"Better that than any of my other habits. Sorry, bad joke." His smirk held a shadow. "I should be glad. Seeing as how money and genetics were my only two contributions, I'm glad he got the good parts."

"Could be worse," she shot back. "All I got from my father was a seventy-eight-inch wingspan."

"Beg your pardon?"

"Sorry, basketball term. My arms measure seventy-eight inches fingertip to fingertip. The bigger the span, the better the rebound potential."

"I take it seventy-eight inches is good."

"Definitely. I'm terrific at rebounding." The phrase's dual meaning hit her then and she started to laugh.

"What's so funny?"

"Inside joke."

"I see." His attention stayed on the road as he spoke, but he might as well have stared straight at her the way her skin prickled, each hair standing on edge. His *I see* sounded way more like *What are you hiding*? What on earth had made her mention her father in the first place?

"Did your dad play basketball?" Ian asked. Again, might as well have been *tell me your secret.*

"So I heard. Do you mind if we turn on the radio?" Running the two sentences together as she reached for the power button, she prayed he would focus on the latter question and miss the first half. She had barely touched the knob when his fingers closed around her wrist.

"What do you mean, so you heard?"

Chloe sighed. So much for her prayers. She stared at the dials, afraid to look upward.

Meanwhile, the car was stopped at a red light, allowing Ian to turn in her direction. The entire left side of Chloe's face warmed from the scrutiny.

Might as well confess the entire sad truth and get things over with. "My father wasn't around when I was born. I've seen him maybe twice, three times in my life."

It took a little courage, but she managed to look Ian in the eye for her next remark. "Needless to say, he never tracked me down to apologize."

Ian let the sympathy in his eyes speak for him. Chloe hated the look. She didn't want his sympathy or his pity. What she wanted was to forget the past. That's all she had ever wanted. To pretend she wasn't the flawed little girl her parents created.

Ian's thumb swept across the top of her wrist, the touch dangerously gentle. "Avoid talk radio, hip-hop, classical, easy listening or love songs and we'll be fine," he said, voice low.

In other words, he would let her share at her own pace. Tightness, sudden and thick, squeezed her throat. "That leaves us with country music," she said, once she managed to find her voice.

"So it does."

Chloe turned on the radio. Seconds later, the sounds of steel guitar filled the interior. It wasn't until she leaned back in her seat that she realized Ian's hand still had her wrist. Jeez, but his grip was sure. So sure it practically melted her bones. Ever since seventh grade, Chloe had been the large one, the girl who loomed over her class-mates and took up more space than she should. Ian's hands, with their large, manly grip, made her feel dainty. Feminine. More feminine than she could ever remember. Worse than that, his touch made her feel significant. It was an unusual and heady sensation. One she could get very used to.

Not to mention scared her to death.

Two hours west, the weather shifted. What had started as heavy rain turned first to sleet, then to freezing rain. All the changes turned the highway into a parking lot. If the odometer could be believed, they'd traveled ten miles in half an hour. "For crying out loud, you'd think people never saw bad weather before," Ian said as the car in front of him flashed its brake lights—again. Thank God for four-wheel drive.

"Funny how icy conditions bring out the caution in people, isn't it?"

Chloe's sarcasm took some of the fight out of him. Some. "I hate wasting time," he muttered.

"Big talk from a man who spends his days sitting around a coffee shop."

"Not sitting, observing," he shot back. "I'm learning the business."

There was a time when he'd barked off people's heads for less. But Chloe's comments simply amused him. He liked how she continued to treat him like a bum. It kept him grounded.

He risked a glance in her direction. Ten minutes into the drive, after he suggested she get comfortable, she'd kicked off her ankle boots and pushed the seat all the

way back. Now she sat with her long legs folded beneath
her in the bucket seat, her plaid wool scarf draped across
her hands and lap like a blanket. His Thoroughbred had
become a kitten.

"Cold?" he asked her.

"A little."

He reached for the thermostat, catching the faint scent
of peppermint as he shifted to the right. He remembered
being amazed by her smell the other night, and wondered
if her skin tasted as minty. The speculation caused his
jeans to tighten.

"Better?"

"Yes. Thank you."

"No problem." Reluctantly, he grasped the wheel
again. He'd much rather keep his hand on the control
panel and continue breathing in the mint, but that would
only lead to trouble. They were friends sharing a drive,
nothing more. "Why didn't you tell me you were uncomfortable?"

"I was told by the driver that he chose the interior
temperature."

So he had, right around the time she'd asked if she
could switch the radio station. "No one touches the control panel but me," he'd told her.

Mint drifted past him again as Chloe shifted in her
seat. Unfolding her legs, she stretched them out as much
as she could and wiggled her toes. No woman should
have such long legs. Between them and her enticingly-
scented skin, how was a man supposed to concentrate
on the road?

Ian suddenly felt her eyes on him, making concentration worse. "Clearly, the media profiles told the truth,"
she said. Out of the corner of his eye he saw her wave her
phone. "Caught up on my internet research."

"I was going to ask what you were doing.... So, what were the articles right about?"

"You having control issues."

"You're only coming to that conclusion now? Wow."

"I had my suspicions before I began reading," she told him. "The article confirmed them."

Confirmed and elaborated, more likely. "I know the picture they painted. Hotheaded micromanager who wouldn't relinquish control."

"Are the articles right?"

"Yeah." And no, too, but he didn't want to get into the whole psychobabble about how he needed to stay on top—stay one step ahead—so he wouldn't screw up and prove his father right. How, little by little, he'd morphed into the old man himself, until he couldn't stand looking at himself in the mirror. Chloe was far too sweet and innocent to dump his dirty past on. Besides, she had her secrets; he might as well have his.

Dammit! When did the driver ahead put on the brakes? Ian slammed on his. At the same time, he shot his arm out to keep Chloe from moving forward. With a loud grinding noise, the antilock brakes kicked in, bringing the vehicle to a stop inches from the other car's bumper.

"You okay?"

"Fine," Chloe told him. Perhaps, but he could feel her chest rising and falling against his forearm. He should have paid closer attention. "You're right about the other drivers being skittish," she said. "It's getting rough out there."

Much as he hated to admit it, she was correct. The farther west they drove, the more conditions deteriorated. Seemed like for every mile the wind velocity gained, visibility lost one. Ian didn't want to say anything, but he'd seen more than one set of lights fishtailing as vehi-

cles swerved on the slippery surface. It served him right
for failing to check the regional weather forecast before
leaving New York. Stupidly, he'd thought that, it being
spring, the frozen weather was behind them.

"Regretting your decision to come along?" he asked

"For the last time, no. If anything, the storm adds to
the adventure."

"Interesting attitude. That why you're squeezing your
seat belt?" He could feel her arm muscles tensing beneath the cloth.

Too bad the traffic demanded his attention and he
couldn't enjoy the color he knew bronzed her cheekbones.
"All right, so maybe I'm a little nervous."

He gave her leg a reassuring squeeze. "We'll be fine."

"I know." The surety in her voice made his heart catch.

"Read a few more articles and you might not feel so
confident," he replied.

"I've read enough. Besides, why would you being a
bastard in business affect your ability to drive?"

"You'd be surprised." Knowing more about his sins
would erase some of the faith from her voice. Her confidence unnerved him. He'd become far more comfortable
with people's disdain.

Give her time. Seriously, how long could he keep her
friendship? Even now, while she smiled trustingly in his
direction, he was focused on how her leg muscles tensed
and released. Every blessed shift made his groin twitch.
A better man would lift his hand away. He wouldn't con-
template sliding it down toward her knee and back along
the inside of her thigh, measuring her length by the reach
of his fingers. What kind of friend did that?

Just then, a gust of wind shook the car. Mother Nature ordering him to keep his hands to himself. Squeezing the leather as tightly as possible, he silently thanked

her for the intervention. "On second thought," he said aloud, "do you still have cell service?"

"Barely. The storm's cutting into my signal, why?"

"Dial 511 and see if you can get a traffic update. I'm wondering if there's more than weather slowing us down."

While Chloe fiddled with her cell phone, he played with the radio tuner. With luck he'd find a local station and get an update on the weather. Learn whether or not they'd be stuck with these conditions all the way to the state university. He'd already ditched any plan of arriving midafternoon. Late afternoon was more likely. Hopefully not much later than that. After all, it was Saturday night. College kids went out on Saturday nights, right? Frat parties and all. Maybe Ian should call his son again, let him know they were coming. For that matter, he should check to see if Matt had returned yesterday's call yet.

"No luck," Chloe announced. "I can't get any signal."

He wasn't having much luck finding a local broadcast, either. The few stations that didn't have static were out of either New York or Philly. "Hope you were serious about adventure, Curlilocks," he said, "because we're about to have one."

He nodded toward the emergency vehicles in the distance.

Oh, yay. Chloe shivered and tucked her scarf tighter around her legs. It wasn't the approaching accident that had her on edge, however, but the way her nerves came to life when Ian's palm rested on her thigh. The touch he'd meant to be reassuring burned through two layers. She swore a palm imprint marked her skin.

Over in the driver's seat, Ian tapped out an impatient

message on the steering wheel. "A lot of flashing lights up there," he said. "Explains the backup."

"Hope it's nothing serious." Chloe spotted red and blue, indicating a variety of rescue vehicles. Tucking her hands beneath her scarf so Ian wouldn't notice, she returned to squeezing her seat belt. It wasn't that she worried about Ian's driving skills—she really did have confidence in his abilities. After watching him take down her mugger, how could she not?

No, she was more nervous that they would stop abruptly and he would fling his arm across her body again. Stupid, getting anxious over a man's touch. But the protectiveness and strength felt so damn good, it scared her.

Drawing closer, they discovered four police cruisers parked facing oncoming traffic. Beyond them, a set of fire trucks surrounded an overturned 18-wheeler. "Looks like she lost her cargo," Ian remarked.

Sure enough, dozens of plastic water bottles were being blown across the pavement, lodging under truck wheels and jamming up against the guardrail. One rolled under the feet of the police officer routing traffic. Poor guy could barely keep his balance in the wind as it was. When the bottle struck his leg, he literally slid several inches. Chloe swore she saw icicles forming on the brim of his hat, as well.

"What do we do now?" she asked, as if she didn't know.

"Follow along and get back on the highway at the next exit," Ian said. "We don't have much choice."

Nothing a control freak hated more than an unplanned game change. While Ian looked calm on the outside, Chloe didn't miss the way his jaw muscles twitched.

"Look on the bright side," she said, "at least the traffic's moving now."

Except the traffic *didn't* move. Half an hour later they hadn't gone more than three miles. Outside her window, Chloe watched as a dead branch fell from a nearby tree. The wind pushed it end over end until it smacked the base of a brightly colored sign. While the limb struggled to break free, Chloe shifted in her seat with a sigh. She knew how the branch felt. No telling how long they'd be stuck in this line. Making matters worse, Ian had turned off the radio, plunging the car into silence. She understood why—he wanted to eliminate distractions so he could concentrate on the stop-and-go traffic. Unfortunately for her, the silence had the opposite effect. Without noise, every breath Ian took became like thunder, every crinkle of his leather jacket a reminder of his proximity.

"La-roo would be miserable," she said. Even if Ian didn't answer, at least her voice made some noise.

"Who?"

"My friend Larissa. She hates cold weather. Put her in a storm like this and she'd never stop complaining."

"Lucky me I'm not with Larissa then. I prefer your attitude."

He was giving her points for not complaining, nothing more. Still, Chloe warmed from the inside out. "How are you doing?" She hadn't forgotten the real reason for their trip: to see his son. All these setbacks delayed their reunion.

"Me? I'm dandy. Nothing I like better than crawling along a country road behind the slowest drivers in America."

"Really? I'd never guess," she said, biting back a smile. "If you like we can switch places. I'll drive and you can be the passenger."

"You're kidding."

The look on his face was priceless. Half horror, half utter disbelief. Chloe let out a laugh. "Don't worry, I'm completely fine with you fighting the roads. I'll just curl up here and enjoy the scenery."

"Such as it is."

She smiled again. Petulance and impatience worked to make his voice rougher. "Are *you* kidding? Have you looked outside?" She pointed to where the same tree branch continued waging war on the same roadside sign. "Where else would you see an advertisement for a place called the Bluebird Inn and—" Ian had flung his arm across her chest again, cutting off the rest. "What...?"

"Another rear end collision. Four cars up. We're stuck while the drivers check out the damage."

"Oh." She'd take his word for it. At the moment, all she could think about was the forearm pressed against the underside of her breasts, and whether or not Ian could feel her heart racing. "What do you want to do?"

He didn't answer. He didn't move his arm, either. Too deep in thought to notice, probably. Taking a slow breath, Chloe gently lowered his hand to her lap. The new position wasn't much better—she'd stupidly let his fist rest between her knees but it beat being wrapped in a faux embrace. "Ian?"

Finally, he shook his head. "This isn't going to work."

"What isn't? The trip?" He wasn't turning back, was he? After they'd come this far?

Rather than answer, he pulled to the right and began inching his way along the side of the road. Ice crunched beneath his tires as they moved up and over frozen mounds of dirt. "Sign back there says there's a restaurant two miles from here."

The Bluebird Inn and Restaurant, the sign she'd been

reading before they stopped. "You want to go to lunch?"
Whatever plan she expected, stopping at a cozy country
inn didn't come close. "What happened to the no side
trip rule?"

"That was before we got stuck in the highway death
march. I figure we'll grab something to eat, and if we're
lucky, by the time we're finished, the traffic will have
eased up."

"And if it hasn't?"

"Then hopefully the inn has internet service so we
can look up an alternate route." He flashed a broad grin.
"See, I can roll with the punches as well as the next guy."

No quick answer came to mind. Chloe was too busy
recovering from his smile.

The Bluebird Inn and Restaurant turned out to be a large
stone farmhouse atop a hill. It took Ian two tries before
their rental car made it up the wooded drive to the parking lot. "Guess we're not the only ones with the idea,"
he said, pulling next to an oversize pickup truck. Sure
enough, there were several other cars in the lot. A few,
like the truck, were covered in ice, indicating they'd been
parked for a while. But the others looked like more recent arrivals.

"Ready to brave the storm?" he asked.

"I thought that's what we'd been doing?" Chloe replied, reaching for her ankle boots. The insides were
warm from being near the heating vent, causing the rest
of her body to shiver in comparison. "These shoes might
have been a mistake, though." The stylish heels were
made for city walking, not ice storms. "Do you promise
to catch me?"

"Why, you planning to fall?"

"I'll try not..." What was that about falling? In the

gray of the rental car, Ian's eyes shimmered like icicles on a sunny day, the pale blue bright and beautiful. Far warmer than their color implied. Chloe found herself thrust back to the other night, as the familiar warmth wrapped tightly around her, the closeness sending her pulse into overdrive. She felt light-headed and grounded at the same time.

Ian's eyes searched her face. Looking for what, she didn't know. Whatever it was, the inspection caused his pupils to grow big and black. A girl could fall into such eyes.

Falling. Right. She blinked herself back to reality. "We—we should probably get moving," she stammered. "Waiting won't make the storm go away."

"No. No it won't." Must have been the left over brain fog making Ian's voice sound rougher than normal as he backed up to the driver's side door.

Snatching her scarf, she tied the square into a make-shift head cover. "I'm ready. And don't worry, I'll do my best to keep my feet on the ground."

A sign on the building said the structure was over one hundred years old. In better weather, Chloe would have been more appreciative of the building's old-world charm. Things like the bright blue storm shutters and match-ing farmhouse door. As it was, she was too busy trying to keep her promise to Ian. An icy crust covered every-thing. Only the fact that the parking lot was loose gravel saved her from wiping out completely. Chloe managed to keep her balance by jamming her heel through the crust into the stones beneath. Her shoes would be ruined, but at least she wouldn't land on her bottom.

They were halfway to the door when Ian's arm wrapped around her. "You look like you're going to top-ple over any second," he said, his breath warming her dampened skin. Chloe fought the urge to curl up close and wind her arms around him in return. Funny, but if she'd been with Aiden or someone else, she wouldn't have thought twice about holding tight.

The front door was painted a vibrant blue. A pair of potted pines decked with white lights stood sentry on either side. Thanks to the overhang, they were the only three items not covered in ice. Ian opened the door and guided her inside.

It was like stepping into another time and country. With its exposed beams and stenciled walls, the room reminded Chloe of an alpine cottage, or what an alpine cottage might look like in her fantasies. The high-back chairs near the window were made for drinking hot cocoa and sketching the world outside, and the aroma...spiced pumpkins and pine. Who knew a room could smell perfect?

A fire crackled merrily in the nearby fireplace. Drawn by the warmth, Chloe walked over and held out her hands. Ian joined her, his leather-clad shoulder brushing hers. "This place is amazing," she whispered, unable to keep the enthusiasm from her voice if she wanted to.

"Certainly beats fast food," Ian replied.

"Tell me about it, although part of me feels like I should head out to the barn to milk the cows or something."

"Well, you do kind of look the part." He fingered the edge of her scarf, which she still had tied like a kerchief.

Chloe ducked her head, afraid to look him in the eye for fear she'd get light-headed again. As it was, his touch was having way more effect than it should. Every brush of his hand, every moment of contact brought with it a wash of sensations. Comfort, attraction, closeness, wariness...

so many feelings she was beginning to have trouble naming them.

"I thought I heard the door."

They turned around to find a man standing at the top of the stairwell. "I am Josef Hendrik. Welcome to the Bluebird Inn."

If the lobby was her old-world fantasy, thought Chloe, then Josef was her fantasy grandfather. Portly and gray-haired with a cherry-colored nose, he wore a beige cardigan sweater that barely buttoned across his torso. He leaned on the banister as he worked his way down to the landing, all the while speaking in a faintly accented voice. "I am afraid, thanks to the storm, both of our king-size rooms have been taken, but we still have a couple nice queen rooms available, one with a view of the field...."

"Actually," Ian said, "we're only here to eat. The sign on the corner said you served lunch."

"Only Sunday through Friday." Josef, who was in the process of sliding his round frame behind the front desk, paused. "I am afraid the dining room is not open to the public until five on Saturdays. You have several hours to wait."

"That's a damn shame," Ian replied. "You sure you can't make an exception? We'd really hate to have to go back outside in this weather."

"I am sorry, son," the man replied. Chloe found the idea of anyone calling Ian son rather amusing. "I wish I could, but thanks to this storm, we are understaffed. It is only my wife tonight, and she has her hands full getting dinner ready for our overnight guests."

"Did the overnight guests get lunch?"

"Of course. The kitchen is always open for them."

"Perfect. Then we'll book a room."

Chloe's jaw dropped as Ian pulled out his wallet.

* * *

"I've dated a lot of guys who called themselves spontaneous, but none of them ever booked a room simply so
we could eat lunch," Chloe said, popping a piece of roll
in her mouth. Of course, none of them could have afforded a room, or if they could, they weren't inviting
her to lunch.

"There was nothing spontaneous about it. I was being
decisive."

"Potato, pot*ah*to." Grinning, she popped in another
piece of roll.

She didn't think it possible, but the inn's dining room
made the lobby look modern. Rustic and romantic, the
room relied on windows instead of overhead light. With
the storm killing all sunlight, candles and firelight filled
the void. As the sole occupants—the other "guests" having already eaten—she and Ian were seated by the stone
fireplace, where the heat warmed the wood and flames
cast shadows across their faces.

The shadowy atmosphere suited Ian almost as well as
the coffee shop. Jacket shed, sweater pushed to the elbows, he seemed to occupy the whole room. That's what
happened when you weren't used to dating men of real
substance; they always appeared larger than life. Not that
he and Chloe were on a date. They were two friends taking a respite from traffic delays.

"Use whatever term you want," her non-date was saying. He wiped his mouth with his napkin. "I saw no need
to go looking for a different place when there was a perfectly good dining room right here. You'll notice they
got us lunch."

Yes, they did. As soon as she and Ian "checked in",
Josef and his wife, Dagmar, wasted no time in making
sure they were comfortable, which in this case meant

serving them big bowls of squash soup and a basket of piping hot rolls. The food was delicious, far better than anything they'd grab at a rest stop.

"More coffee, Mr. Black?" Dagmar came out of the kitchen brandishing a coffeepot. Unlike the innkeeper, she was decidedly not Chloe's fantasy grandparent. No grandmother of hers would look like an aging film star. Dagmar brushed a stand of her silvery-blond hair from her face. "I just made a fresh pot."

Ian matched her smile. "Don't mind if I do. Lunch, by the way, was delicious. I appreciate you opening the kitchen for us. I know you've got to get ready for dinner."

"No trouble at all," she said with a flutter of her hand. "The pleasure is mine. If you need anything else, you let me know, yah?"

"Absolutely. I will do just that." He was using the same lazy growl he'd used the day Chloe had met him, the low silk-on-sandpaper voice meant to wrap around a woman's spine. Apparently it was his charm voice.

And Dagmar was definitely charmed.

"Looks like you've won a fan," Chloe said, once the older woman had sashayed back to the kitchen. "And here I thought you were famous for being difficult to work with."

"Doesn't mean I can't be charming when I need to be."

"Obviously."

He raised an eyebrow. "Is there a problem?"

"Of course not." Chloe could hear the sharpness in her voice and it bothered her. What did she care if Ian flirted with some middle-aged innkeeper with perfect hair? It wasn't as if that growl was reserved solely for her. "I was wondering how long you want to stay."

He was busy checking his cell phone. "Not too much

longer. I noticed Josef had a laptop. I'll ask him to check the local weather and traffic before we leave."

"Doesn't look like the storm's let up much," she noted. In fact, conditions appeared worse. They could hear the wind howling from where they sat.

"Hopefully, we're looking at more rain than ice farther west."

"And if we aren't?"

"Then, Curlilocks, we get to see if you turn into a pumpkin."

A shiver ran down Chloe's spine. He was merely making a joke, and a silly one at that, since he mashed together fairy tales. The setting, however, along with his ragged-edged voice made the words sound like a seductive promise.

Ian was checking his phone again, staring at the screen with a frown. "Something wrong?" Beyond current circumstances.

"I left a message for Matt yesterday. I thought he'd have called back by now."

"Did you ask him to call?"

"No, not outright."

"Well, no wonder then." They'd entered her area of expertise now: rationalizing silent phones. "How else would he know he's supposed to call?"

"I would."

"You're different."

Ian settled farther back in his chair. "Exactly how am I different?" he asked, his eyes shining in the firelight.

"You're..." The words coming to mind at the moment—*special, unique, amazing*—weren't ones she wanted to share aloud. Mainly because the fact that she would use such words to describe a man frightened her.

"You were a CEO," she said finally. "You're used to having people at your beck and call. Your son is a college freshman. My experience with guys his age is you have to lead them step by step through everything. And even then they might not get the message."

"When I was eighteen, I was in the army. A higher ranking officer asked and you said yes." Ian's current position had him in the shadows, making his expression difficult to read. Chloe swore she saw a frown. "Come to think of it, I ran my company in a similar fashion."

She was right; she did see a frown. "You go with the world you know."

"I suppose you do."

Silence followed. In the car, the silence had closed everything in. Here, in the empty, half-lit restaurant, quiet felt more like distance. It brought a sadness to the air.

Chloe reached to draw him in again.

"How's Dagmar's coffee? Better than yours?"

His chuckle made Chloe happy. "Don't be ridiculous. We use far higher quality beans."

"That so?"

"You don't notice, since you insist on killing the taste with peppermint and chocolate syrup."

"Hey! You should be nicer to one of your best customers."

"The best," he corrected, leaning into the light. "Not to mention one of my favorites."

What on earth made her think the air had chilled, when Ian was studying her as if she were the only female on earth? A woman could get damn addicted to a look like that. She might even start believing it to be true.

Getting an internal grip, Chloe did what she did best, and acted unaffected. "Just one of? I must be slacking. What's a girl got to do to make top of the list?"

"What makes you think you—"

She was what? Not at the top? Or had a chance? The questions went unanswered as a loud crash suddenly shook the entire building.

CHAPTER SIX

You've got to be kidding. Ian stared at the giant tree covered in power lines lying in the driveway. Clearly, nature had a sick sense of humor, because the monstrosity managed to block both the road and passage off the property.

As soon as the crash sounded, Ian, Josef and several other guests rushed outside. They stood in a clump halfway down the hill, surveying the damage.

"Tree's been dead for years," Josef said. "I told my neighbor he should call someone to cut it down, but looks like the weather did the job for him."

"Looks like it took power along with it," one of the guests commented.

Sure enough, cables laced the limbs like thin black snakes. Behind them, the farmhouse sat dark, a victim. Ian peered through the trees, searching for light, and saw none. "From the looks of things, the tree took out the whole street when it fell," he said.

Josef's sigh spoke for all of them. "Telephone, too. Hopefully, I can find cellular service so I can call for a road crew."

"Good luck getting a truck out here," a different guest said. "We had a storm like this in Connecticut a couple years ago. Took days before they cleared all the damage."

Peachy.

Above them, pine branches groaned. Instinctively, the entire group looked upward for debris before taking a few steps backward. "Tell the crew I'll double their rate if they get here as soon as possible," Ian told Josef.

"That is very generous of you."

"Generosity has nothing to do with it." He was eager to get on the road, and if money helped bump the inn to the top of the list, he was more than glad to pay.

Top of the list. He'd been about to say the same thing to Chloe when the tree saved him. He was beginning to wonder if she wasn't a test, as well. With her curls and her infectious smile, not to mention those mile long legs, the woman was temptation in high heel boots. He'd been celibate for almost as long as he'd been sober, and for the first time, the lack of companionship ate a hole in him. When he'd wrapped his arm around her waist in the parking lot—hell, before that, when they'd sat in the parked car—images of what he'd gone without had flashed through his head. Beautiful Technicolor images of tawny skin spread out beneath him.

The scariest part of all was his attraction wasn't only physical. She had this way of drawing him out from behind his facade. In one day he'd shown her more of himself than he had anyone, short of the addiction counselors.

Worse, he had this inexplicable desire to know more about her. Like what secrets lay behind that false bravado, for example. A trait so much like his it hurt. But then he thought about all the women whose hearts he'd broken, and he reminded himself he had all he could do to keep his own life together. Complications like Chloe, as intriguing as she was, would only lead to more mistakes.

"You must be psychic."

Ian pulled out of his thoughts to find Josef smiling at him. "How so?" he asked.

"Booking a room. Looks like you will need to stay the night."

Images flashed before his eyes again. Oh yeah, definitely a test. "About that," he said, following Josef and the others to the house. "Do you have a second room available?"

"Really? I assumed…" The innkeeper looked surprised. "The two of you look quite comfortable together."

Sure, if *comfortable* meant being perpetually half-aroused. "Is there a second room?"

"Of course," Josef replied. Ian ignored his disappointment at the man's answer. "I'll do up the paperwork soon as I check to see Dagmar's got the generator running."

"Thank you." That was one test taken care of.

Good thing, too, because Chloe insisted on meeting him at the entrance with a mug of steaming coffee. Wordlessly, she held it in his direction.

"You read my mind," he said.

"In this case, it wasn't so hard to do." She turned on her heels and headed back indoors, but not before shooting him a smile that made his stomach take a strange, hard tumble.

Gripping the mug like a lifeline, Ian watched her walk away. Definitely a complication, he thought to himself. A damn fine complication. He headed off to make sure Josef remembered that second room.

"Extra towels are down the hall. We also keep a supply of toiletries on hand—shampoo, toothbrushes and other essentials. I will check to see if Dagmar has an extra nightgown you can borrow as well."

Somehow Chloe didn't think petite Dagmar and she took the same size, but she appreciated the gesture. "Thank you."

"Do not give it a second thought. Our house is your house."

So long as they were paying customers. Only a couple hours earlier he'd wanted to turn them away. Her fantasy grandfather was quite the capitalist.

Josef filled her in on a few more details, such as where she could find an extra blanket, reminded her that guests could get coffee twenty-four hours a day, and headed off in search of sleepwear, leaving Chloe alone for the first time since their arrival.

First time since this morning, really. She threw herself on the bed. As she lay there staring at the ceiling, her mind automatically went to Ian, who'd stayed downstairs to finish his coffee. His mood had shifted between when he'd left to check out the storm damage and when he'd returned. Lunch's good humor had disappeared. Shouldn't be surprising, seeing how this trip had been nothing but delay after delay. Now they were stuck here for goodness knows how long. The control freak in him must be ready to scream.

Rolling on her side, Chloe took a good look at her surroundings. The room was gorgeous. Small, but filled with all sorts of cozy extras, like fluffy robes and a pillow-laden window seat. Of course it helped that, to save a strain on the generator, Josef had provided her with a battery operated lantern. The light's glow mimicked candlelight in the wake of the setting sun.

An emptiness filled her chest. The Bluebird had been created for couples—real couples, like Del and Simon or Larissa and Tom. She was an outsider amid all the romance, a fact that Ian drove home when he'd reserved a second room. Nothing reminded a woman she was alone like a man sleeping in his own bed.

You'd think she'd be relieved by Ian's gallantry. She

knew plenty of guys who'd assume because they were together, they could share a bed, whether sex was involved
or not. Ian respected her privacy—further proof he was
different. Sadly, it also made him that much more attractive. It was Chloe's pattern of inverse relationships: The
more disinterest, the more attractive. Seriously, though,
how could a woman not find Ian Black attractive? Funny,
smart, considerate, sexy Ian Black. La-roo was right;
Chloe had been fooling herself to think otherwise.

A soft knock sounded on the door. Josef and his never-
fitting nightgown, no doubt. "That was fast," she said,
opening the door.

"I'm a fast drinker." Ian smiled from across the thresh-
old. His cheeks were still ruddy from being outside, the
bright pink adding to his virility quotient and causing
her stomach to tumble end over end.

"I thought you were Josef," she said, gripping the
molding for support.

"Sorry to disappoint you."

"You didn't." She dug her fingers into the wood. Nothing like blushing in return. "I mean, is there a problem?"

"While I was finishing my coffee, I saw a large branch
blow off a tree in the backyard. Got me worried."

"About what?" They'd already lost power and telephone service. What more could the wind do? Topple
over the building?

"This," he said, producing a garment bag.

"My dress!" With everything going on, she'd forgotten it lay in the backseat.

"Figured it'd be safer hanging in your room. The way
today's going, I didn't want to chance a tree falling on
the rental car."

She was touched he remembered. Gathering the bag
in her arms, she went and hung it on a hook on the back

of the closet door. "Seems like you're forever rescuing pieces of my wardrobe."

"Just don't tell me you owe me. Being stuck here for the night already makes us pretty even."

"Alright, I won't." She unzipped the bag. The dress was still in perfect condition, the azure silk barely wrinkled.

"Pretty gown," Ian said. She could feel him hanging by the door, watching.

"Told you I got a banging dress out of the deal."

"Interesting color."

"Apparently it's Simon—the groom's—favorite shade. I'm only glad the color looks good on me."

"I'm betting most things look good on you."

There he went, making her feel special again. "You've never seen me in bright pink," she murmured, zipping the garment bag shut. Actually, he had, because she was pretty sure her cheeks were that very color. Why did he have to say such nice things?

Josef's voice saved the day. "Turns out Dagmar agreed with you about her nightgown not fitting." The innkeeper appeared in the doorway holding a plaid flannel shirt. "She suggested this. I hope it will suffice."

"It'll be perfect. Thank you." Out of the corner of her eye, Chloe caught Ian trying to fight a smile. "Don't say a word," she warned him once Josef had left.

He did, anyway. "Sexy."

The shirt was faded Black Watch plaid, soft and comfortable looking, but sexy? Not so much. "Whadda you know? There are things I don't look good in."

"Who said you wouldn't look good?"

Chloe had to ball the shirt in her fist to keep her stomach from tumbling again. "Well, you'll never know, will you?"

Hearing herself, she nearly winced. The comment made her sound disappointed, which was the last thing she wanted him to think. Quickly, she stuffed the garment under a pillow and changed the subject. "Thank you for booking a second room." There, that should erase any notion that she expected more. "It was very considerate of you."

"I'm not so sure I'd use the word *considerate*," he replied.

No, he'd probably use *no-brainer* or *common sense,* wouldn't he? *Considerate* implied a deeper relationship. She should stop before she dug herself into a deeper hole.

Fluffing her curls, she moved across the room. "Thank you again for rescuing my dress."

"Wasn't much of a rescue. All I did was carry the thing upstairs. It's not like I saved you from a mugging or something."

"Very funny." He'd brushed off that act with modesty, as well. "For the record, I know a lot of guys who wouldn't have even remembered the dress was in the car, let alone gone out in a storm to retrieve it."

Ian gave her a long look. Such a long look she found herself fidgeting. With nothing close by to play with, she settled for tracing the slope of the footboard with her palm.

"Maybe you should start dating a better class of guy," he said finally.

Yeah, well there was the rub. Better class guys didn't want her. They rented separate rooms. "Or quit dating," she quipped. Just her luck, the light tone she'd hoped for failed to materialize.

"Little young to close the book completely, aren't you?" he asked, sitting on the edge of the bed.

"Am I?" As far as she was concerned, it all depended

on your perspective. A lifetime of guys walking away more than made up for her age.

Ian's eyes had yet to stop looking at her. The scrutiny reminded her too much of the other night when the air grew intimate and unsettled. Taking a seat on the other side of the bed, she grabbed one of the pillows and set it on her lap in an attempt to increase the distance between them. She never should have said anything in the first place.

"I'm sorry your trip's been delayed," she stated, fingering the piping.

"Not as sorry as I am." Gratitude washed over her. As he had in the car, he was letting her change the topic.

Mirroring her actions, Ian grabbed a pillow, too. The Hendriks clearly didn't believe in skimping when it came to bed decorations. "Logically, I know one day's delay won't make a difference."

"But you can't help but feel time is ticking away while you're stuck here."

"Exactly."

He looked surprised. If only he knew. Chloe understood exactly what he meant. Eventually there came a tipping point, when the bitterness became too much to overcome and all the apologies in the world wouldn't make a difference. For a man like Ian, so used to being in control, the idea that such a time might be near would be terrifying. "Your son's still young, though," she assured him. "Plus, didn't you say the two of you have already connected?"

"Yeah…" The sentence was incomplete and she knew he was thinking about Matt's unreturned call.

"Hey," she said, leaning across the bed to get Ian's attention. "It'll be all right. The two of you are already talking. Plus, don't discount the fact you were there for him financially all these years. That matters, too. You could have ignored him or forgot he ever existed."

Too late she realized what she'd said. Stupidly using *forgot* instead of *pretend.* Naturally Ian picked up on the slip. "Is that what happened to you?"

"Sort of."

"What do you mean?"

Chloe ran an index finger across one of the circles decorating the bed's quilt, wishing she might find an answer hidden in the calico. How did a person explain that their father didn't want them without sounding pitiful?

The bed sagged, and a moment later she felt Ian's breath on her forehead. He'd joined her in stretching out across the bed until they lay head to head in the middle. His index finger brushed across her wrist. "Chloe?"

Looking up, she saw his eyes only inches from hers. Up close, the blue wasn't nearly as pale. Tiny pearl-gray lines sprayed from the center, giving the color depth and dimension. He waited for her answer with such sincere interest, she had to look away before her own eyes teared up.

"I told you my father wasn't around much," she began. "What I didn't tell you is that sometimes we'd go years without a word. Soon as we convinced ourselves he was really gone for good, he'd show up again. Somehow, some way he'd convince my mother to take him back, and for a couple of days, maybe a week, they'd be all hot and heavy. Until he took off again."

"Must have been hard for you, not knowing if he was staying or going."

"I guess. Mostly I tried to keep out of the way."

She went back to tracing the comforter, the pattern easier to deal with than the sympathy in Ian's eyes. Might as well tell him the rest of the sad story. "Last time I saw him was on my sixteenth birthday. My mom must have finally had her fill, because she met him on the front walkway and sent him packing. I haven't seen him since."

"Oh, Curlilocks..."

Ian's thumb brushed across her cheekbone. If she'd been crying, he would have been wiping away a tear. Fortunately, she'd stopped crying over her father a long time ago. Still, she closed her eyes, indulging in the warmth the gesture brought to her insides. "You know what I remember most about the visit? Not that my mother kicked him out, but the fact he didn't bring a present. I don't think he remembered it was my birthday. Anyway, that's when I knew."

"Knew what?"

That she wasn't worth the effort. "That my mother had terrible taste in men." Chloe meant for the comment to sound flip, but like so much of her conversation today, the tone missed the mark.

Ian's palm continued cradling her cheek, the warmth of his touch drawing her in. "Your father was an idiot," he whispered.

Oh Lord, if only he knew how badly she wanted to believe those words. To hear him whisper them... The sentiment went straight to her heart. All the pent-up longing, the wishes she so carefully kept locked away behind a breezy facade, threatened to break free.

It was too much. Too comforting. Abruptly, she sat up and brushed at her eyes. To her surprise, they were damp. "What matters is you're not forgetting your son. When he finds out you've been attending—"

"You don't need to pretend...."

"Pretend?" She pushed the curls from her face. "I don't know what you're talking about."

"Yes, you do. You don't have to put on this act as if

what happened with your father is no big deal, when we both know it is."

Busted. She hated how he seemed to see a deeper part of her. Even so, she wasn't about to admit the truth, not when she was so practiced at denying. "What makes you think I'm pretending? My father's been gone for over a decade. Plenty of time for me to process his behavior and the fallout." And if she hadn't…? Who wanted to listen to someone whine about the father who didn't love her. There were plenty of people with more pressing problems. People like Ian, whose amends were the reason she was on this trip.

Outside the wind howled, reminding them they weren't going anywhere that night. Scooting to her feet, she went to the window, only to stare at her own reflection. "Wonder what kind of damage we'll see when we wake up," she mused.

"Hopefully minor. Although I have to say the ice looked pretty thick when I was outside earlier. Going to be a real mess now that the temperatures are dropping again."

"Well, at least my gown is safe."

"Which is what's important." She watched his reflection as he propped himself on one elbow again. "Maybe you should wear it to dinner tonight. Show up the other guests."

"What a great idea, and if I'm really lucky I can spill gravy down the front of me. I think I'll stick with what I'm wearing."

"I guess that means the flannel shirt's out, too." She could see his grin in the glass. He looked so relaxed and at home, sprawled across the bed. As if they should be sharing the space together.

But they weren't. The thought hadn't even crossed his mind.

"I think I'm going to freshen up before we eat," she said, turning around. "Do you want me to knock on your door when I'm ready to go downstairs?"

He sat up, and for a minute she swore he seemed disappointed at being asked to leave. A trick of the low light. The shadows caused everything to look off. "Sounds good. I'll see you then. Hopefully you'll change your mind about the dress…"

"Nice try."

"I'll see you in about ten minutes. And Chloe?" He paused in the doorway. "My father stuck around. Isn't always a good thing."

It was just a glimpse, a sliver to let her know she wasn't the only person whose past had left them scarred. It might have been the best present she ever received.

As soon as the door closed behind him, the room grew cold from his absence. Chloe stole one more look at the rumpled spot on the bed where Ian had lain, before turning back to the glass. Minimal damage, Ian had wished for. He'd been talking about the storm. Why did Chloe have the feeling she should be more worried about the damage being caused inside?

CHAPTER SEVEN

WHY THE HELL did he share that last bit about his father? On the list of topics never to be discussed, the old man owned numbers one through infinity. Yet the comment had slipped right out, easy as pie. *My dad stuck around. Isn't always a good thing.*

God, but it was way too easy talking to Chloe. Listening to her kick herself about her own loser father compounded the problem. It certainly said a lot about the man's quality—or rather his lack of quality—when Ian looked admirable in comparison. Chloe had appeared so lost while telling her story. He'd wanted to wrap her up in his arms right then and there, protect her from all the lousy men in the world. Seeing how he was one of those lousy men, however, he'd held back.

And shared the tidbit about his father instead, giving verbal comfort instead of the embrace he preferred. From the spark in her eyes, his offering was appreciated.

She was waiting in the hallway when he stepped out of his room. Winter coats did nothing for women, that's all he had to say. Day after day, he watched her march to the counter, her long form masked by winter bulk, and the whole time she hid a body made for handling. Thank heaven spring was right around the corner.

"Decided against the dress, did you?" he teased, drink-

ing in her length. Not that he minded the jeans and turtleneck, but he would have enjoyed seeing her wrapped
in silk.

"Sorry, you're stuck with me as is."

"As is isn't so bad, either." She rewarded his compliment with a very attractive blush. Better looking than
the silk, he decided.

"You shaved."

"Yeah, I decided to look civilized for dinner." Another
uncharacteristic move. He preferred uncivilized as often
as possible, but for some reason, when he'd stepped out
of the shower and saw the shaving gel and razor by the
sink tonight, he got the urge to clean up.

"Don't worry." He ran a hand across his chin. "The
stubble will return soon enough. I've been blessed with
a tenacious five o'clock shadow."

"And here I thought you just liked looking rough-
and-tumble."

"Who says I don't?" he asked, winning himself another blush. The woman's cheeks colored on a dime; he
liked it.

There were already guests in the dining room when
they arrived. During lunch, he'd considered the empha-
sis on flames and natural lighting over the top, but this
evening the lighting looked perfect. If he hadn't spent
hours driving in the ice, he'd never know there was a
storm outside.

"Glad you could join us," Josef greeted. "Seat yourself. Thankfully, the generator is running without problems, so we will have our regular menu. Unfortunately,
we are short on servers so there will be a few delays."

"Thank goodness for generators," Chloe murmured
once they'd walked past. "I was wondering if they'd be
able to serve hot food."

"Hot food and hot toddies, from the looks of things," Ian replied. Josef hadn't been kidding about being short staffed, either. The innkeeper himself was running around with a heavy pewter pitcher, topping off patrons' mugs. "You know what they say; a little whiskey makes any delay palatable. Would you like one?" He started to raise his hand to signal Josef.

"You wouldn't mind?"

"You having a drink?" He shook his head. "Much as I'd like it to, I can't expect the world to stop on my account. Besides, I've got a replacement vice."

"Dagmar's coffee. How could I forget? I think I'll pass, anyway." She slipped her hand around his wrist.

Ian could let her touch his skin all night. Such long, graceful hands. Before he realized what he was doing, he'd pressed the tip of his index finger to hers. "I see what you mean about wingspan." Her fingers were nearly as long as his.

"You mean my gigantic man hands. Perfect for palming the ball."

"I don't know about that, but those are not manly hands. Trust me, I know a lot of guys."

"Thank you." To his disappointment, she pulled her hand away, back to her side of the table. "For the record, though, I did have mad ball-handling skills."

"I believe you, Curlilocks." He was sure she could handle a lot of things well. Grabbing his water glass, he took a long drink, wishing the unwanted sentiment out of his head.

Silence settled over the table while they studied the menu. Or rather, Chloe studied the menu. Ian couldn't take his eyes off her. It wasn't that she looked any different. Sure, she'd touched up her makeup a little and combed her hair, but she was essentially the same woman who'd slipped into his car this morning. And every bit as alluring. "Know what you're getting?" he asked, breaking the silence before his assessment grew out of hand.

"You mean from the menu option of one?" she replied.

Looking down at the paper before him, he saw it described a set four-course meal. Fortunately, Chloe mistook his question for sarcasm. "Guess asking for a burger is out of the question."

"You've got to love a good hunk of meat."

And a woman with simple tastes.

Suddenly, he noticed her frown. "Is this the same table we sat at for lunch?" she asked, looking around.

He'd been caught. "What can I say? I'm a creature of habit." More like a creature who enjoyed the way the flames colored her skin from this angle, and wanted to watch the transformation again. "Blame my rigidity on the army."

"How long did you serve?"

"Eight very long years."

"I take it you didn't enjoy military life."

"Enjoy?" He shook his head. "The army is all about team building. One big unit working toward a common goal. I'm not exactly a team player."

"Let me guess. You didn't take orders well, either."

Coming from anyone else, the comment would have made him bristle. "Guilty as charged."

"Then why did you…"

"Enlist?" Did he dare share more? Tell her how it was either enlist or let his father suck what little life he had left out of him? The mood was too pleasant to spoil with the dirty truth. "I didn't have a lot of options. School wasn't a choice, and neither was sticking around."

He cast a quick glance over the top of his water glass

and was nearly done in by the understanding in her eyes. No explanation was necessary. "I stayed to prove a point."

She cocked her head. "A point?"

"That I could stick it out." *You won't last two weeks in the army. You'll be right back here like the nothing you are.* He didn't want to talk about those days anymore. "What matters is I lasted long enough to know I'm better at giving orders than taking them."

"Not to mention figuring a way to make the world a better place," she replied.

It was the first time anyone had suggested he made anything better. "You're going to have to explain."

"Your blood coagulator. If you hadn't gone into the army, Ian Black Technologies would never exist."

"Oh, that." Guilt, his old friend, tapped him on the shoulder. Here's where he started letting her down.

"What do you mean, oh, that? Your product has saved countless lives."

No doubt, and there were days when he was damn proud of the product. The product, not himself. "You know I'm not the one who actually created the coagulator patch, right? All I did was pull together the people who did the work for me." To make money. To prove another point.

"In my business, we call that person the idea man. Every successful business needs one."

Until it didn't need him anymore. Or until the idea man became drunk and volatile and his own worst enemy. Ian grabbed his water, quickly washing the sour taste out of his mouth.

Once more, Chloe mistook his action. Grasping her own glass, she saluted him. "And now you're saving the world again," she said.

"How's that?"

"You said yourself that without coffee, man would kill himself. You're saving lives with high quality beans."

The gloom he felt creeping over him receded in a flash. "I like the way you think, Curlilocks. You're good for my ego."

"Good. When you become a big-time coffee magnate and need an agency, make sure you hire CMT and give me credit. That way I can score points with Simon."

"Simon, as in Simon Cartwright?"

"You know him?"

Yeah, he knew him. Or rather *of* him. Apparently, they possessed similar tastes in women. "We had a few…mutual acquaintances."

"Is that society-speak for dated some of the same women?"

He could feel the color creeping up his neck. "I wouldn't call me the society type." Certainly not like Cartwright, who, if Ian recalled, had been born to the roll. "But yes."

"In other words you're a serial dater."

"Interesting term." Sounded fatal. Considering the stack of apologies he'd written, the word was spot on.

He sat back in his chair. "I suppose I have dated my fair share. Hard to be monogamous when your soul's focused elsewhere."

"You mean drinking."

Sure. Let alcohol take the blame. Even if the liquor was only a by-product of a bigger demon.

"Not that I'm judging," Chloe continued. "By Delilah and Larissa's standards, I'm every bit as bad. But then they're overly romantic right now."

"Aren't all new brides?"

"I don't know about all, but those two certainly have taken the lovesick pills." She reached for her water. "I keep trying to tell them not everyone in the world has a soul mate. Statistically, it simply isn't possible."

"Because there isn't an equal number of men versus women."

"Exactly!" She saluted him with her glass again, her eyes glittering as though she'd proved some great scientific theory. So flushed and gorgeous, he had to squeeze his goblet to keep the blood from rushing below his belt. "You do realize there are more men than women in the world, right? Meaning men are the ones on the short end of the soul mate stick."

Chloe's smile faded. "Thanks for killing my theory."

Great, he'd gone and dimmed the sparkle. Why the hell did he have to say anything? Because the idea of her spending her life alone wasn't cause for celebration, that's why. Any notion that involved a woman like her being alone wasn't.

"You will, you know," he said. "Find your soul mate, that is." Wouldn't be someone like Aiden, either.

"You assume I'm looking for one."

"You aren't?"

"Let's just say I'm going to leave the veils and flowers to people like Delilah and Larissa."

That so? "Even though statistics are back in your favor?"

"Statistics aren't the only reason." Her smile was as indecipherable as her answer. Didn't matter. She could toss out all the nonchalant, enigmatic comments she wanted; he didn't buy a single one.

After eating, most of the guests either went back to their rooms or headed into the living room for an after dinner drink. Ian, however, leaned close and whispered, "Feel like exploring?"

Seeing how his question wrapped around her spine like a naughty suggestion, Chloe should have said no. The reckless side of her took charge, however, and she leaped at the offer.

Josef had told her the Bluebird's history when he was showing her to the room. The original structure dated back to the Civil War, while additions were added over the years based on the owners' needs. As a result, the first floor was a crazy pattern of rooms and hallways.

"Should we tie a string to one of the doorknobs in case we get lost?" she asked Ian.

"Where's your sense of adventure, Curlilocks?" he teased. "Besides, the place only looks confusing because the lights are out."

Precisely her problem. She wasn't sure if Josef and Dagmar were trying to reduce strain on the generator or discourage guests from roaming, but the rear of the inn was dark except for some isolated night-lights and lanterns. "Aren't these people worried about law suits?" she asked, tripping over a raised floorboard.

"Don't worry, I'll catch you if you fall."

Would he? She'd made him make the same promise in the parking lot this afternoon, only she wasn't sure she meant literally anymore. Ever since their conversation in her room, her insides felt like one of the wind-tossed trees outside.

It hardly helped matters that their conversation over dinner had further strengthened the connection she felt toward him. Nor did it help that he stood so close to her she could smell the wool of his sweater.

They rounded a corner and came to a small reading room.

"This must be the library Josef mentioned," Ian said.

As was the case in the other rooms, the lights were

off, leaving a small fireplace as the sole source of illumination.

"How many fireplaces are there in this place?" Chloe asked. "Must take forever to light them all."

"Maybe, but you won't hear me complain."

"Me, neither," she hastened to assure him. "A night like this one screams for a warm fire." And the flames were far too inviting. She held up her hands. The heat burned her palms, causing the rest of her body to shiver from the temperature difference.

"Cold?" Ian appeared near her shoulder.

Chloe shook her head. "I like firelight, is all. You know, that's how I started going to your coffee shop."

"We don't have a fireplace."

"No, but your walls are fire-colored. All the red and orange—very warm and appealing."

"I had no idea. And here I thought you came in because of Aiden."

Aiden. Those days seemed so long ago. "He's why I started going so often, but I first walked in because of the decor."

Spying the fireplace set, she picked up the poker and began moving the logs around so the flame would burn brighter. "Blame the visual artist in me—I'm attracted to bright colors. There's something about them that's very....welcoming. Like fireplaces."

"Remind me not repaint, then. I wouldn't want you to feel cold."

He was joking, but the comment still made her tingle from the inside out. She gave the logs another poke. Sparks popped and floated upward. "You really want me to stay warm in your café, turn the heat up a couple notches."

"Let's not get carried away. I said I wanted you warm,

not the whole damn customer base. How about I loan you another sweatshirt instead?"

"One's enough, thank you. A second would require another mugging, and I think I've had my fill."

The fire burned brightly now. Content, Chloe gave the log one last poke, then set the implement aside, as Ian squatted down next to the hearth.

"You're right," he said. "The fire does feel nice."

"Doesn't it? Too bad we don't have marshmallows we could toast."

"We could always raid the pantry. See what kind of secret stash they keep in there."

Chloe plopped down next to him. "Not much of a raid when you've got the hostess wrapped around your little finger."

"What makes you say something like that?"

"Oh, I don't know…how about 'Do you want more coffee, Mr. Black? How do you like the crème brûlée, Mr. Black? I hope the meal met with your standards, Mr. Black.'" With each "Mr. Black" she imitated the woman's lilting Scandinavian accent. The innkeeper had been very solicitous.

"She was simply being a good hostess."

"Toward you, maybe. I had to wait twenty minutes for my iced coffee. In fact, the only reason I got served at all was because she wanted to bring you a refill."

"Now you're just exaggerating."

"Am I, *Mr. Black*?"

A small smile threatened the corners of Ian's mouth. If Chloe didn't know better, she'd say he was purposely trying to goad her. "I suppose it's possible the woman recognized my name and was a little impressed."

"If you say so, although…" It was Chloe's turn to do a little goading of her own. "…I don't think it was your name she was staring at when you walked to the men's room. Unless that's what you're calling your behind these days."

Ian laughed. The carefree sound made Chloe's heart give a tiny bounce. "How would you know she was staring at my rear end? Unless you were watching, too?" He gave her shoulder a nudge.

"I was simply following her line of sight."

"Uh-huh."

"Seriously. I was not staring at your rear end." Actually, she was, but she certainly wouldn't admit it to him.

"Too bad," he replied. "Because then I could feel less guilty about staring at yours."

Chloe did a double take. "You were not." When did he have the opportunity? When she'd gotten up to use the ladies' room? "No way."

"You'll never know, will you?"

He was mimicking her comment from upstairs, although in his case, the words sounded far sexier. Then again, she was pretty sure he could read the fine print on a contract and make it sound sexy. Her skin grew hot. She couldn't help herself. Every compliment, implied or otherwise, took up residence in her chest, leaving the space between her heart and lungs so full it was hard to breathe.

Suddenly, the atmosphere shifted, and what had started as lighthearted grew still and expectant. The mirth disappeared from Ian's gaze, replaced by a new light, hot like the center of a flame. Outside, branches slapped at the house as trees bent and swayed to nature's will. Looking into Ian's eyes, Chloe swore she was bending and swaying, too.

"Dear God, but you're beautiful," she heard him whisper. His knuckles brushed across her cheek, the feather-light touch making her shiver. "Thank—"

His kiss swallowed the rest.

A whimper caught in Chloe's throat. It was a slow, sensual kiss, full of passionate promise.

Her eyes fluttered closed. He tasted like coffee, and the small part of her brain still working realized she would never think the same way about the beverage again.

"Oh! I did not realize anyone was in here."

Josef's voice broke the spell. Ian's arms dropped away, leaving Chloe swaying for purchase. As she struggled to regain her composure, she swore her ragged breathing was the only sound in the room. Frankly, she wouldn't be surprised if they could hear it on the upper floors— along with the sound of her racing heartbeat.

"I was coming in to check on the fire before heading upstairs," the innkeeper said. From the way he hovered in the door frame, he didn't know whether to complete his task or not.

Ian was the first to recover. Shooting Chloe an indecipherable look, he turned and smiled at the innkeeper. "Go on upstairs. We'll take care of the fire."

"Well, if you are sure…" He, too, gave Chloe a look, which she returned with a weak smile. Hopefully the embarrassment creeping up her spine didn't show too much. Being caught necking in a darkened room. Talk about awkward.

Especially since the kiss felt like way more than mere necking. Making out had never left her aching with such need before. It was as though her soul had woken up from a long nap she hadn't realize she'd been taking.

"All you need to do is close the glass door. The fire will burn out on its own."

"Will do," Ian told him.

Unable to voice anything more than a whisper, Chloe gave a small wave goodbye. Her heart had yet to slow down. If anything, her pulse kicked up another notch as soon as Josef disappeared around the corner. She turned back to Ian, expecting to find a desire to match.

His face was shuttered. "I...it's been a long day."

No need to say more. She wasn't good enough for a serial dater. Why make the moment worse with a whole lot of false apologies and excuses?

At least now she knew how to take all his implied compliments. "You're right," she said. "I should be heading upstairs. See you in the morning?" The hopeful note that sneaked in at the end of her question made her want to kick herself.

Ian nodded. "I'm not going anywhere."

True. They were stuck together until this trip ended. And she'd thought Josef walking in on them was awkward.

Straightening to her full height, she turned and walked away. It took effort, but she managed to reach upstairs without running. She'd be damned if she'd let Ian see how much his rejection hurt. Her blood pressure might shoot through the roof, but she would spend the rest of this road trip with a smile on her face. What she didn't understand, she thought while brushing her teeth, was why he'd kissed her in the first place. Some kind of game? A challenge? Or was she remembering the moment incorrectly, and she'd been the one who'd made the first move?

Whatever happened, it was her fault for letting her guard down. Something about being with Ian had her opening up about parts of her life she never shared with anyone else. For crying out loud, she'd told him about her father!

As if she wasn't disgusted by herself enough, she took a good look at her reflection upon donning the flannel shirt. She looked like a plaid circus tent with legs.

And swollen, thoroughly kissed lips.

Dammit, Ian. Stepping back into the bedroom, she found her attention going straight to the rumpled spot on the comforter where he'd lain earlier. He'd looked so comfortable stretched out there. So weirdly...right.

It was an image too good to be true. For her, anyway.

For the first time in eighteen months, Ian rolled out of bed cotton mouthed, and lucky him, he hadn't had to drink to get it. No, he'd earned the bleary-eyed state by spending most of the night thinking about the woman next door. The woman he had no business kissing, but had kissed anyway. Might as well have been alcohol, because once he started, he didn't want to stop. Thank heaven for Josef. God knows what might have happened if he hadn't shown up.

Ian pictured the disappointment that had flashed across her face when he'd stepped away. If only she knew how hard it was.

Once his body cooled down and common sense returned, he'd realized just how smart it was for him to stop. Maybe if she'd been some mercenary socialite... but she wasn't. She was sweet and funny. His past was already littered with good women who'd offered their hearts, only to discover he was incapable of returning their feelings. He didn't want Chloe to become one of them.

Man, though, could she kiss.... He could still taste her, still feel how her long lean body had ground against him.

He groaned aloud. Thinking about last night did not help. If he was back in New York, he could distract himself with the paper while watching the staff brew the first pots of the day. Lying here, he had too much access to his thoughts.

It was the quiet that had woken him. All night he'd listened to the pelting of freezing rain against the glass. There was no rain now. No wind, either. The only sounds Ian could hear were those of birds chirping.

A tug on the window shade revealed a mottled sky of blue and gray. The storm had left damage, though. The entire world was coated in ice. Branches, cars, even the sides of a work shed glistened as part of a frozen wonderland. Fortunately, he saw some of the branches already beginning to drip. This time of year, ice never stuck around long. The downed tree in the road was a far bigger problem. It couldn't be moved until the power company cleared the lines. Who knew how long that would take? Chloe and he could be stranded here another night.

He ignored the thrill that arose at the thought.

Yanking on his jeans and sweater, he headed downstairs in search of coffee. If this place kept its promises, then a pot would already be brewing. Otherwise, Josef and Dagmar would have to deal with him making his own.

Chloe's room was silent as he walked by. Nice to know one of them could sleep following last night. As he passed, he ran a hand across the door's painted surface, a poor substitute for Chloe's burnished gold skin, but probably the closest he'd come to a caress again.

"Good morning!" Josef stepped through the front door as Ian reached the landing. "You are up early. Did you sleep well?"

Ian gave the man credit; he acted as though last night's awkward encounter had never happened. "Very well, thank you," he said, playing along.

"Glad to hear it." The man propped a hiking pole against the wall, then hung his jacket on a wooden hook. "I was spreading salt on the front steps. If you and your friend go for a walk this morning, you will need to be careful. Until the sun warms everything up, the ground is an ice skating rink."

"Any word from the power company?" Ian asked.

The innkeeper joined him at the buffet and poured himself a cup of coffee. "I called this morning and got a recording that said they had crews on the job. Unfortunately, I also heard on the radio that there are power outages all over the state. Forty thousand people without power, I think they said. Even with your generous offer, I have a feeling repairs will be a while. I hope you were not in too much of a hurry to leave."

"Would it matter if I was?" Ian asked.

"Not really." Josef offered him the creamer, which Ian declined. "I noticed your car has New York plates. Were you coming or going?"

"Going. My son is a student at the state university. We were heading out to see him."

"What a shame you were unable to make the trip. But I am sure your son will understand."

"Hope so." The man had no idea how much. As Ian stared at the black contents of his mug, he wasn't so sure.

Behind him, the stairs creaked softly. "Good morning," Josef greeted. "I wondered if you would be joining us at this hour or not."

Ian's body tensed in awareness. Without turning around, he could tell who it was Josef spoke to. His insides sensed her approach.

Sure enough, when he turned, Chloe stood on the bottom stair.

He'd been wrong to tease her about the flannel shirt. The oversized garment looked sexy as hell on her—even with the jeans she'd tugged on to cover her legs. Soft and flowing, with a wide neckline that revealed the honey-colored skin around her neck. His body tightened as he remembered just how that skin tasted.

She'd pulled her curls into a topknot, but a handful of corkscrew tendrils had managed to work their way loose. It was those she brushed at with her hand before offering a small wave. "Good morning," she replied.

She smiled as she joined them, but Ian could tell it was for Josef's benefit only. The corners of her mouth were pulled too tightly, and while her eyes avoided looking directly at him, he still caught the embarrassment shining in their depths.

"Hope there's enough coffee left for me," she said, turning to their host.

"Why, of course. Allow me to pour you a cup."

"I thought you preferred to drink iced coffee," Ian remarked. He hoped the innkeeper took the hint and went to get some ice so the two of them could have a moment alone. Chloe, however, must have known what he was doing.

"I've been known to drink both. Besides, if you add enough milk, the coffee cools down fast and it's almost like iced."

"Almost but not quite."

"Close enough." She took the cup Josef offered and began adding what amounted to a second mug of cream. All to avoid standing alone with Ian. So much for friendship. He wanted to kick himself.

"Ian and I were just talking about the two of you spending an extra night."

The knuckles on the hand gripping her mug handle tightened. "Is that so?"

"All our guests will, unless we can get the tree moved by the end of the day. At the moment, it does not seem likely."

"Josef, can I get your help in the kitchen?" Dagmar's voice called out.

The innkeeper drained the rest of his coffee. "The boss beckons. I had best see what she wants."

"Will you be coming back?" Chloe sounded so nervous, Ian's stomach dropped.

"Afraid not. When Dagmar signals she needs help, it is usually the end of my spare time for the day. I will let you know when breakfast is ready to be served. Hope you two like eggs because we have a lot of them to cook up."

"Farm fresh eggs," Ian remarked. "Don't see those every day."

"No, I suppose you don't."

Chloe's smile had vanished along with Josef. "Another day, huh?" she said, staring at her mug. "You must be disappointed."

"A little." At the moment, he was more disappointed that she continued to avoid his gaze. Unable to stand her evasion any longer, he caught her chin with his forefinger, forcing her to look in his direction. The apology in her eyes tore his guts out. "We need to talk."

CHAPTER EIGHT

BUT NOT IN the main salon. There were too many oppor-
tunities for interruption. Before Chloe could say a word,
Ian grabbed her hand and led her down the hall to the
first empty room and shut the door.

She blinked in disbelief at the unlit fireplace. Star-
tled as she was by Ian's abrupt maneuver, it took her a
minute or two to realize they'd returned to the library.
"I didn't think you'd feel comfortable going upstairs,"
he explained. "And this way we can speak in private."

"Do we have to?" If he wanted to talk about last night,
Chloe would rather not talk at all. She'd spent enough
time rehashing the evening while not sleeping.

"I think we do."

That's what she was afraid he'd say. She took a seat on
the edge of the leather sofa, while Ian stayed by the door,
arms folded, leaving miles of distance between them. As
she waited for the inevitable "it's not me, it's you" litany,
she struggled to keep from tugging at her neckline.

Wearing the flannel had been a mistake. That they
both knew she'd slept in the shirt left her feeling more
exposed than the wide-open collar. Exposed, foolish and
a thousand other adjectives. Didn't matter that Ian had
yet to look her in the eye, choosing instead to focus on a
spot on the floor; she still felt naked.

"I owe you an apology," he said.

"No, you don't." *Please don't,* she added silently. Apologizing meant he regretted kissing her, and she didn't want to hear the rejection out loud. No matter how confused her thoughts, she needed to believe he'd wanted her, even if only for a moment. "You kissed me and I kissed you back. End of story."

Well, the end except for the fact that her skin still burned where his lips had touched her, and that staring at him this morning, she ached for him to kiss her again.

He lifted his eyes. Chloe immediately wished he'd go back to staring at the floor. "I had no right—"

She couldn't do this. Couldn't sit and listen to his excuses. "Look, we're both adults." This time, she held up her hand. "Last night was…We got caught up in the atmosphere after a stressful day. It happens. There's no need to make a federal case out of it." Considering how her insides were trembling while she spoke, she applauded herself for sounding so mature.

"Are you sure? I don't want things to be awkward between us."

"They'll only be awkward if you keep apologizing for something you don't need to apologize for." Or that she wanted to hear him apologize for. Hearing the note of relief in his voice was hard enough.

Besides, she realized there was some truth to her statement. Between their conversations and the storm, yesterday had been an emotionally draining day. They probably did overreact to the romantic atmosphere. Things between them would be much different now that the sun was out.

If he would stop studying her, that is. With her hand clutching at her open neckline to cover herself, she rose and walked to the window. On the other side of the glass, a sparrow hopped from shrub to icy shrub. Chloe watched, grateful for a distraction. "Believe me," she told Ian, "if you needed to apologize, you'd know. You'd be wearing a cup of coffee."

There was no missing the relief in his chuckle. "Lucky me, then, since I don't have a spare shirt."

Before she could blink, he'd joined her at the window. Leaning on the sill, he stretched his long legs in front of him. "Far as I know, only the cars in the parking lot are stuck here. The rest of the street should be fine."

Chloe frowned. "What does that mean? You planning to buy someone's car?"

"Nothing that drastic, but I was thinking there's got to be a train station within a town or two. I could walk up to one of the neighbors. See if they'd be willing to drive you there."

So he could ship her back to New York. "You want me to leave?" She was surprised by how much the suggestion hurt. She'd rather have the apology.

"This was supposed to be a one-day trip. I've already derailed your weekend. There's no need for you to miss work, too."

"I appreciate you thinking of my career."

"And your friend's wedding. We're assuming they'll have the tree cleared in twenty-four hours. Could take longer. Don't you have maid of honor duties to do?"

Yes, she did, and his arguments made sense. There was absolutely no reason to stay if she could find a way back to the city. Better yet, he was offering her a way to escape the romantic fishbowl they'd found themselves in. Seeing how the sun was shining and his nearness still ignited a longing sensation in her chest, heading home might be a good idea.

Except...in laying out his argument, he'd left out a

very important reason, perhaps the most compelling of all. "Is this what you want?" she asked. "Do you *want* me to go back to the city?"

"You've long since paid me back for the purse snatching."

She'd forgotten that's how the trip began. At some point between New York and this morning—the moment she'd slid into the passenger seat of his car, most likely—obligation had stopped playing a role. "Maybe I want to see this trip to a successful conclusion."

"What about your friend the bride?"

"Delilah? She'll be fine. So, if you'd like me to stay, I will."

If Chloe hadn't been holding her breath, waiting for his response, Ian's slow smile would have taken it away. "I'd like that," he said in his sandpaper whisper.

Her heart did a little victory dance. "Good."

Turned out Delilah wasn't fine with the decision. "What do you mean you're stuck in Pennsylvania?"

"Long story." Chloe took a few steps away from the building. With the storm over, she'd discovered she could get a faint cell signal by standing on the back patio, and so she'd called to update her friend. "I'm here to give Ian moral support."

"The guy from the coffee shop? Are you nuts? You barely know him."

And yet Chloe felt as if she'd known him forever. "I know him better than you think," she said aloud.

"Seriously? Three days ago you thought he was an unemployed slacker."

Only three days? Wow, it seemed so much longer. "Since then I've learned a great deal more about him."

On the other end of the line, Delilah sighed. "You've

done some crazy things, Chloe, but this…? Going away for the weekend with the man?"

"We planned on it being a day trip. Just long enough to drive to the state university and back."

"Awful long way to go for a day trip."

"He wanted to visit his son. They've been estranged for years, and this was the first time they would meet in person. I thought he could use the support."

She chewed her lower lip and waited. Delilah knew enough about her past that she didn't have to say much more. "Does he appreciate the gesture?" her friend asked after a moment.

Chloe thought about the smile she and Ian had shared in the library. "I believe he does.

"Look, I know what I said the other day, but he's not at all the guy I thought he was. In fact, he's very…" Sexy. Funny. Incredible. "He's nice."

"You like him then."

"Of course I like him. I just told you he's a nice guy. Why else would I agree to take an eight-hour car ride with the man?"

"That's not what I meant."

"Nothing romantic is going on. Ian's not—that is, neither of us are interested in romance."

"Never stopped you from falling before," Delilah replied. "In fact, isn't 'disinterested' a job requirement?"

"Very funny." Just once she wished her friends didn't pay such close attention to her behavior. "You're as bad as La-roo, you know that?"

"We try."

"In this you can stop trying. I can guarantee nothing's going to happen." Ian had made it quite clear. "You can pass the message along to Larissa, too. I don't need her calling and gushing about some potential romance that isn't."

"I will, if I can reach her. She hasn't answered her phone all weekend, either. Maybe she and Tom got stuck in the storm, too."

"Either that or the two of them are spending the weekend reading the hotel brochure for the thousandth time. Or making little doohickeys to give away to the wedding guests. Did I mention I'm grateful you don't worry about those kinds of details?"

"Right now the only detail I'm worried about is whether I'll have a maid of honor. Promise me you won't run off to Hawaii with your new boyfriend until after the ceremony, please?"

"I promise," Chloe replied, refusing to comment on Del's using the word *boyfriend*. "Besides, I spent way too much money on that dress not to walk down the aisle."

A few minutes later, she clicked off the phone with a sigh. Something Del had said disturbed her. Not when she called Ian her boyfriend—that was typical teasing—but earlier. *That's never stopped you before.*

"Ow!" An object smacked her head. Looking up, she saw that pieces of ice were falling from the tree. All around her tiny chunks were melting on the patio. Funny how quickly things could thaw. By evening, much of the ice would be gone. Already, the same frozen crust that she'd had to jam her heel into yesterday to cross had turned to slush.

Voices sounded from the driveway. Picking her way across the parking lot, she found a circle of male guests staring at the tree in the road, pointing out other large branches that littered the area. It was easy to find Ian in the group. He was the most masterful figure there. How on earth did she ever think him a slacker?

One of the men said something, causing him to laugh. The throaty sound reached her insides despite the distance, lodging in the center of her chest like a warm fuzzy ball.

Delilah, annoying as her comment was, had a point. When it came to men, the more disinterested, the more attractive Chloe found them. Ian, with his sexy smile and his insistence that he wasn't made for a relationship, fit her bill perfectly. He was exactly the kind of guy she chased.

So why did being with him feel so different than the others?

The question nagged her most of the day. Actually, a bunch of questions nagged her. How was it that being with Ian could feel as natural as breathing, while at the same time scare the heck out of her? Made zero sense. No wonder she'd told La-roo she needed a break from the dating world. Clearly, the whole Aiden catastrophe had left her brain fried.

"So this is where you've been hiding."

Chloe jumped, her pencil skidding across the paper on her lap. Ian stood propped against the door frame, arms folded across his chest. As usual, her insides took a dive roll the moment she saw him.

"Who said I was hiding?" she said, brushing some stray curls off her face. Stupid topknot wouldn't hold them all. "Since you and all the other male guests were busy surveying storm damage, I figured I'd come upstairs to take a nap, is all."

"You always nap with a pencil and paper?"

"Obviously, I'm not napping at the moment." She'd tried, but her thoughts wouldn't let her relax. "I found some scrap paper in the desk and decided to do some sketching."

"Really? Can I see?" he asked, stepping into the room.

"Um…" She looked at the papers in her lap.

What started as a sketch of the pines had turned into a series of doodled logos for Ian's coffee shop. "Sure. Why not?"

She handed him the designs. "For me?" he asked, surprise in his voice.

"I was goofing around with some ideas. Nothing serious."

"I like them. The middle one especially. The lettering isn't hitting me, but the concept is right."

"What if I…" She grabbed the paper back and quickly rounded off the letters, giving them a more fluid look. "That work better?"

"Like you read my mind."

She tried not to take the comment seriously, but her heart beat a little faster, anyway. "Then your mind must be easy to read," she told him, pushing the feeling of connection aside.

"Funny, but my old employees never said so. Then again, I was half in the bag most of the time, so mind-reading would have been difficult." He went back to studying the sketches.

Chloe pulled her knees closer to her chest. It dawned on her that his honesty regarding his drinking bordered on self-abusive. "Why do you do that?" she asked him.

"Do what?"

"Mock the fact you had a drinking problem." Listening to him put himself down the way he did hurt. "Shouldn't you cut yourself a little slack?"

"Should I?" he countered. "Have you forgotten why we're on this road trip?"

"Doesn't mean you should beat yourself up."

He let out a long breath. "You're a sweet kid, you know

that?" Before she could protest the kid label, he sat down on the arm of her chair. "I have to mock," he said. "It's the only way I can get past what a bastard I used to be."

"Used to be," she reminded him. "You're not a bastard now."

"That's because you're seeing me on my good days."

If he meant to warn her off, the attempt didn't work. "I still think you're being too hard on yourself."

He smiled and brushed her cheek with the back of his hand. "You'd think differently if you saw the damage I caused. My list of amends is pretty damn long."

At least he was making amends. To her, that's what mattered. Although she doubted he'd believe her.

She settled for changing the subject. "You never did explain why you picked coffee for your next business adventure."

"I didn't?"

Chloe shook her head. "Care to share now?"

"Do you want the public relations version or the truth?"

He stretched his arm across the back of her chair. What started as his being perched on the arm suddenly turned into a crook with her nestled close to his chest. "Truth, please," she replied.

"I like coffee."

Chloe waited for the rest of the answer. When one didn't come she started to giggle. "Seriously?"

"Deadly. This way I can control my vice."

"You want control? I'm shocked."

He poked her shoulder. "Speaking of control, the power company arrived. They're busy clearing the downed wires as we speak."

"That's great. You must be happy."

"I am." Strangely, his voice lacked enthusiasm. Chloe chalked it up to nerves.

"Of course," he continued, "clearing the wires is only the first step. We still need to cut the tree into sections and move it from the road."

"We?"

"I convinced a couple of the other guests that if we did the work, the job would go faster than if we relied on Josef and the neighbor across the street—who, by the way, is older and about half Josef's size."

Chloe laughed at the description. "Sounds like a wise decision."

"We thought so. If all goes right, the road will be clear by early evening. We'll be able to head out west first thing in the morning."

Bringing an end to their stay at the Bluebird Inn. She was surprised at how disappointed the thought made her feel. You'd think she'd be relieved, given that, contrary to what she'd told Ian, she'd spent the day hiding from him.

"Sounds terrific," she told him. "Thanks for finding me and letting me know."

"Actually, giving you a road update is only part of the reason I was looking for you."

"Oh?" Drawing her knees close, she swiveled in her seat so she could look up at him. "What's the other part?"

"To tell you I have a surprise planned for after dinner."

"A surprise? For me?" Images of last night's kisses flooded her senses, making her pulse race. "Why?" *Please don't say to make up for last night.*

"Because…" She wasn't sure if he paused to think of the right words or if he changed his mind about answering altogether. "A guy can't do something nice for a friend?"

Friend. The word didn't fit as right as it once had. Friends didn't make her insides ache with longing.

"Truth is," Ian continued, "I wanted to thank you for coming along with me this weekend."

"We've already been through this. You don't have to thank me."

"Stop spoiling the fun."

"Sorry. The gesture just caught me off guard." After all, surprises were reserved for couples, not *friends.*

"You're supposed to be caught off guard," Ian replied. "That's why it's called a surprise."

He grasped her chin, tilting it up until their faces were so close Chloe thought for a moment he might kiss her again. "Six-thirty in the dining room. Don't be late."

Don't be late? How could she possibly? She would be counting the minutes.

Much to her chagrin.

"No peeking, now."

Chloe felt Ian's lips against her ear. "Your eyes are closed, right?"

"Sealed tight. Is this really necessary? I feel a little silly." Not to mention anxious. Ever since Ian had mentioned an after dinner surprise, she'd been a bundle of anticipatory nerves, and now, with her eyes closed, the expectancy had her other senses hyperaware of the man propelling her forward. Ian's hands rested on her shoulders, the pressure of each finger finding a way through her turtleneck to excite the nerves beneath. She felt his broad chest hovering behind her. She could even sense the soft knit of his sweater brushing up and down her back as he breathed.

It was probably time for her to accept that she'd gone and done exactly as Delilah predicted: fallen for Ian.

Never one to take your own advice, were you, Chloe?
Much as she hated to admit it, she was hopelessly and
deeply into the man.

"Relax," he said, mistaking her tension for self-
consciousness. "No one's here to see you."

True enough. As soon as the road opened, most of the
guests had piled into their cars and headed home, leaving Chloe and Ian the only couple left. As a result, the
two of them ate dinner with Josef and Dagmar. The arrangement only added to Chloe's nerves, since she had
to spend the entire evening pretending not to notice the
knowing glances being shared around the table.

Ian turned her body to the right. "Ten more steps,"
he told her.

"You counted?"

"Of course. We wouldn't want you tripping and falling on your face, would we?"

"Ah, that means we're heading someplace with ob-
stacles."

"Maybe." His voice appeared in her ear again, low and
rough. "Then again, for all you know, I could be mess-
ing with you."

In more ways than one. She swore that, with every
step, his body moved closer to hers.

One of Ian's hands left her shoulder, and a moment
later she heard the click of a doorknob. A soft gust struck
her face; a door being pushed open.

Two steps forward and the air temperature suddenly
changed, becoming warmer. Chloe heard the sound of
crackling wood. "Is that a fireplace?"

They were in the library. Last night's kiss flashed before her, stirring a heat she was afraid to let take hold.

"Okay, open your eyes."

She blinked, adjusting to the darkness. Someone had

moved the furniture. Pushed the sofa and chairs toward the wall. In their place lay a large tablecloth, the bright red square spread in front of the fireplace like a picnic blanket. At the far corner, she saw a silver tray bearing a tea set and several covered serving bowls.

She arched a brow. "A picnic?" This *was* a surprise. She didn't see Ian as the picnic type, let alone a picnic by firelight.

"Not any old picnic," Ian replied, taking her hand. He motioned for her to sit, then reached for the tray. "I'll have you know, by the way, I worked extremely hard on this." Based on his grin, Chloe couldn't tell if he was serious or making a joke.

He lifted the first cover. Chloe slapped her hand over her mouth to keep from laughing. "Oh my God, you raided Dagmar's pantry!"

"More like charmed her into setting this whole thing up," he replied. "Told you I worked hard."

She bet. More likely Dagmar had caved at the first smile.

One by one Ian uncovered the dishes, revealing marshmallows, graham crackers and chocolate squares. "You said you never cooked s'mores over an open fire before, so I figured…"

He'd give her the opportunity. Chloe stared at the tray in disbelief. It'd been a casual comment, babble really, nothing more, and yet he'd listened. The men she knew didn't care about any of her life's details. They certainly wouldn't go to this much trouble to help her live out a childhood fantasy.

Attraction shifted into an emotion she couldn't name. The strange feeling filled her chest, squeezing her lungs. Her vision blurred.

"Hey, hey, hey." Ian moved to her side. "There's no need to cry. They're only marshmallows."

"I'm not crying. I'm..." She blinked the tray back into focus. "I can't believe you did all this."

"Dagmar did the work. All I did was smile and say please."

They both knew he'd done more than that. It was wonderful. *Sweet, wonderful...* Words couldn't describe the fullness in her chest, so she settled for wrapping her fingers around his, hoping the connection would speak for her. "Thank you," she whispered.

"My pleasure, Curlilocks."

With his free hand, he brushed her cheek, and Chloe wondered if he felt the inadequacy, too.

"Ian..."

He broke away. "Enough with the thank-yous," he said, reaching for a skewer. "We have marshmallows to toast."

For the next few minutes, they sat cross-legged in front of the fire, watching as the flames licked their marshmallows brown. When the surface of hers began to bubble and expand, she let out a giggle. "This is already better than using the microwave," she told him.

"You are way too easy to please."

"I wouldn't be so sure. If this tastes as good as I anticipate, then you will definitely have to install a fireplace in the coffee shop."

She pulled the crispy, gooey confection off the end of her skewer and popped it into her mouth.

"What happened to the rest of the steps? Aren't you suppose to stack them all together?"

Mouth full of marshmallow, Chloe shook her head. "Didn't want to spoil the toasted flavor."

"Terrific. I made Dagmar unwrap all those candy bars for nothing."

Laughing, Chloe sipped her hot cocoa. "A woman never lets chocolate go to waste." To prove her point, she picked up a piece. The square had turned soft in the heat and she had to lick the remains from her fingers.

She was running her index finger over her lower lip when she heard a soft hiss. Looking up, she found Ian's stare glued to her mouth, his gaze hot and needy.

It was the *needy* that did her in.

They moved as one, their bodies coming together in a tangle of mouths and limbs. Last night's kiss promised passion, tonight's delivered. The moment Ian's lips slanted across hers, instinct took control. They moved in sync, until even the sound of their breathing shared a rhythm.

And then, suddenly, Ian broke away. Swearing, he buried his face in the crook of her neck. As she listened to his breathing, Chloe continued to hold him tight. Her head was spinning. What had happened?

Swearing a second time, Ian lifted his head. "Do you have any idea how many times I promised myself I'd quit drinking before I actually went to rehab?" he asked.

Rehab? Why on earth was he talking about drinking now when he could be kissing her? Chloe was about to ask that very question when she caught the anguish in his expression. The question clearly mattered.

She shook her head. "How many?"

"Too many to count. I'd promise, and fifteen minutes later I would toss my resolve out the window. And do you know why?"

Again, Chloe shook her head.

"Because I'm a stubborn bastard who always has to have his way. Makes resisting temptation very difficult," he added, brushing the curls from her eyes. Chloe felt his fingers tremble as they moved across her skin.

He wasn't talking about drinking. He was talking about kissing her. "It's not temptation if we both want something," she told him.

His laugh was hollow at best. "If only it were that simple."

"Maybe it is," she replied. "Maybe we're simply over-thinking."

"Or not thinking at all." Sighing, he rolled away, his departure causing Chloe to shiver. "You're a sweet kid, Curli, you know that?"

Kid. He'd said the same thing this morning. It was, she realized, his default answer whenever things turned inti-mate. As if using the term helped him keep his distance.

"I'm not a kid," she reminded him. "I'm a grown woman."

"I know." He shot her a look that would melt steel. "Believe me, I know."

"So, I don't understand. What's the problem?" Any other man would be leading her to his bedroom by now. "Is it me?" Of course it was. Stupid question.

His horrified expression was little comfort. "Oh sweet-heart, no."

She wanted to believe him. She did. "Then...?"

"Because I like you."

Her heart stuttered. Ian rose and walked toward the rear window. "I've got a list of amends a mile long," he told her, looking out into the darkness. "Do you have any idea how many people I've let down over the years?" What he was really saying was *how many women.* "I don't want to see you dragged down, too."

"In other words, you're being noble." Funny, for a rejection—and a clichéd rejection to boot—the words went straight to her heart. Call it wishful thinking, but his expression reflected in the glass looked so regretful it made her feel special rather than cast aside.

Pulling herself from her paralysis, she joined him by the sill, her heart cringing when he looked away. Up close, she saw traces of self-reproach mixed with his regret. Further proof of his sincerity. This time it was she who brushed his cheek. Her silent way of telling him nobility wasn't necessary.

"You deserve—"

"Shhh." She didn't want to hear the protest. Not when, right here, right now, she knew there wasn't anyone in this world better than the man next to her. They'd been dancing around this moment all weekend; both of them afraid of what would happen if they let their guard down. She was tired of being afraid. She wanted him. Wanted him in a way that went far beyond sex.

"I've got all I need right here."

In case he didn't believe her, she forced his gaze to meet hers. Every muscle in his body was tense, shaking from restraint. In the shadowed blue light, she saw the desire struggling to break free. "Right here," she repeated, and brushed a kiss against his lips.

A groan tore out of his throat and he wrapped an arm around her waist. Chloe found herself yanked tight against his body. "Do you have any idea how difficult you are to resist?" he growled.

The roughness in his voice turned her insides raw. "Show me," she challenged, her rasp matching his.

He did.

CHAPTER NINE

CHLOE LAY ON her side watching Ian breathe. Sleep managed to do what consciousness couldn't, and that was to erase the stress from his face. He looked younger, less burdened. She traced the planes of his face in the air above him, down over the curve of his shoulder and along the scar on his arm. The raised cord was the only imperfection on his flawless body. She followed along to his wrist, ending at the hand splayed next to his pillow. One hand from a pair that had so masterfully played her body. While she wasn't as experienced as she often pretended to be, she recognized a skilled lover.

Why then, if Ian was so amazing, was she wound tighter than a drum?

You know why. Ian was different than other men. Waking up and seeing him lying next to her felt way too natural. He inspired words like *complete*, *real* and *forever*. Scary, troublesome, dangerous words—at least for her. She felt as if she stood on the edge of a steep cliff, one with the lip pulling away from beneath her feet. Every instinct told her to take a few steps back.

But then she'd remember last night, not the lovemaking, but the fullness that had gripped her heart when Ian revealed his surprise, and the words took hold again.

"You look a million miles away."

She started at the sound of Ian's whisper. Pulling away from her thoughts, she looked over and caught the gleam of his eyes as he watched her in the dark. "What time is it?" he asked.

"Four o'clock."

"What are you doing awake? Everything okay?"

The darkness made the concern in his voice sound urgent. So much so that for a second, she worried he'd heard her thoughts. "Fine," she lied. "Couldn't get comfortable is all. I didn't mean to wake you."

"You didn't. I wasn't sleeping all that well to begin with." He scrubbed his hand over his face, his strangled sigh loud in the darkness. "Too much on my mind, I guess."

Regrets? Her insides steeled, ready for rejection. "Anything I can do?"

"You've already done more than enough," he replied, rolling to his side. "In fact, you've been pretty darn incredible."

Chloe fought the urge to burrow under his arm. Afterglow compliments were no doubt standard operating procedure for a man with Ian's experience, and he still managed to say the words with such tenderness, her insides melted. "Are you trying to make me blush?" she asked, grateful for the darkness.

"I do like the color your skin turns." He nuzzled her curls. "I knew," he murmured against her temple. "From the minute you walked in wearing those high heeled boots, all curls and attitude. I knew you'd be a force of nature." He pulled back. "Why do you wear those high heels?"

"So the world will see me coming." And be forced to acknowledge her existence.

"You're very hard to ignore." She felt him smile. "Even

before you tossed your iced coffee. Now—" he gave her a quick kiss "—how about we see what we can do to make you more comfortable."

Rolling on his back, he wrapped an arm around her shoulder and pulled her close. She nestled into the crook of his arm, burying her face against his neck.

"Better?" he asked.

"Definitely."

It was her second lie of the night. Being in Ian's strong embrace wasn't better; it was *the best*. Once more, the words she feared danced before her eyes. *Complete. Real. Forever.*

Something was off, Ian thought as he pried open his eyes, and it wasn't the empty expanse on the other side of the bed or the sound of the shower.

In point of fact, it was *exactly* those two things, along with the tightness in his gut when he noticed them. Usually, on mornings after, he was the one up early, looking for a drink and a way out.

Perhaps that was why he felt so unsettled. Not only had he given in to temptation—enjoying every blessed second, he might add—but here he was, lounging in bed without any inclination to move.

The shower stopped, and a few minutes later, Chloe stepped into the room wrapped in a towel. As soon as she spied him, she flashed a smile. "You're awake. I was afraid I'd have to throw cold water on you."

Still might, he thought, adjusting the blanket. There was way too much honey-colored skin on display. Pushing into a sitting position, he pretended to lounge against the headboard until he could get this body under control. It was a lost cause. As Chloe bent over to scoop her clothes from the floor, all hope vanished. Man, he really did suck when it came to resisting temptation.

"Actually, I'm surprised I slept as late as I did. Guess all that tossing and turning at 4:00 a.m. caught up with me."

"I hope it wasn't because I used you as a pillow."

"Curli, you using me as a pillow was the second best part of the night."

There it was, that gorgeous pink blush. The same color her skin turned when she was aroused. "Last night was pretty...um..." She bent to retrieve a stray sock. "What time would you like to leave?"

"Leave?" The hem of her towel had risen, affecting his concentration.

"I'm assuming you must be eager to hit the road so you can see Matt."

"I am." Unsure where this conversation was going, he drew out his answer. The way her eyes were glued to her clothes rather than on him gave him pause. "Why do you ask?"

"No reason. While I was in the shower, I got to thinking that maybe..." She crumpled the sock in her fist. "Maybe I should have you drop me off at the train station, after all."

"What?" He sat up straighter. "I don't understand. When I asked you yesterday, you didn't want anything to do with the idea."

Why the one-eighty?

"Yesterday you were talking about hiking through the ice and asking a total stranger to drive me. Now that you're back to driving, the situation is different.

"Besides," she added, "you're going to want privacy when you talk with Matt. I'll only be in the way."

Mostly I tried to stay out the way.... Why did that comment pop into his head?

"You would have been in the way Saturday, too. That didn't stop you from tagging along."

"Saturday was before…"

They slept together. Of course. Typical Chloe with her bravado. She was trying to act casual, something she was clearly not accustomed to doing. Guilt stabbed him in the gut. *You selfish bastard.*

"Don't be ridiculous. I want you there," he told her. Finally, she showed her face. With her clothes clutched to her chest, she eyed him warily. "You sure?" she asked.

"Positive," he replied. So much so, it shocked him. "But first, there's someplace else I want you." Drawing back her side of the covers, he patted the mattress.

Chloe's eyes widened. "I thought you were in a hurry to see Matt?"

"We've got plenty of time, Curli. Plenty of time."

He'd forgotten how big the state university was. Driving onto campus felt more like entering a small city. It didn't matter if it was raining; students still roamed everywhere.

Just as Ian turned a corner, a flash of red rushed by his driver's side window. He sucked in his breath, only to realize it was a false alarm.

Chloe shifted in her seat, reminding him he wasn't alone. "We played in a tournament here once. I remember the girls from their team were Amazons."

Picturing her long, muscular legs, he smiled. "Like you should talk."

"I was downright petite in comparison, thank you very much. Did Matt text you?"

"Not yet." Ian had sent a message before leaving the Bluebird. "He's probably in class." He ignored the lump in his stomach determined to remind him it'd been three days since the first call, with no word.

"What are we going to do then? The campus is a little big to simply wander around asking if anyone knows Matt Black."

"Only place we're going to wander to is the president's office. I'm sure with a little persuasion we can get ahold of Matt's schedule."

She stared at him. "In other words, you plan to buy your way around the privacy rules."

"Hey, perks of being rich." If only his insides matched his outward confidence. The closer they got, the more he wondered if this plan, which had made such sense in New York, was going to work.

A familiar silhouette near the center of the parking lot caught his eye. Driving closer, he discovered the boy had brown hair. Another mistake.

He parked and let his forehead drop to the steering wheel.

"How are you holding up?" Chloe asked.

Holding up? His stomach was stuck in his throat. "I keep seeing kids I think are him," he told her. Of course, the odds of Matt simply walking by were slim to none.

"You'll see him soon enough," she said.

"I know." The thought made his pulse race. Thirteen years was so very long. "What if it's a mistake?"

"What are you talking about? Of course it's not a mistake."

"No, I mean being in his life at all. What if..." Ian struggled against the fear rising up inside him. "What if he's better off without me?"

"He's not," Chloe said. "He's going to want his father in his life."

She believed that because of her own father. "Not all dads are worth having. Mine was a miserable drunk."

"You are worth having."

Damn, did she have to speak with such assurance? "You don't know that," he said, shaking his head.

He turned his wrist so their palms faced each other, and entwined their fingers. The connection calmed him. He thought of how many times and ways she'd comforted him this weekend. Now he was about to lean on her once more. She should hear the whole story, though. "I didn't build Ian Black Technologies to save lives. I built it to make a fortune. So I could rub my success in my father's face. Nothing else mattered. *Nothing*."

Years of working nonstop. Drinking and working. Leaving the people who cared because he was too drunk and too driven to give them what they needed.

"I wanted so badly to prove him wrong," he said, staring at the rain-covered windshield. "Instead, all I did was prove I was as miserable a bastard as he was. What if being around me does the same thing to Matt?"

Slowly Ian turned to face her, expecting reproach. Instead, he saw a sheen in her eyes brighter than ever before. "It won't," she whispered.

"How do you know?" For crying out loud, he'd hurt so many people on his way to the top. How could she possibly be so certain still? Especially after what he'd said.

"Because." She cupped his cheek. "You're different. You're better."

Ian let the silence settle around them while he sat holding her hand. What did he do to deserve her crossing his path? She'd been a gift, his Curlilocks. The kind of woman a man could not only draw strength from, but who he could go toe-to-toe with, as well. A challenge and a comfort. If only he'd met her earlier. Before he'd crashed and burned.

"Ian?" Brown eyes shimmered with concern.

"I'm sorry," he told her.

"Sorry for what?"

For leaning on her so much, for pretending he didn't notice her casual air this morning was a little forced, for being selfish. Any of those answers worked.

What he said was "For suggesting we find a way to send you home Saturday. I…" He squeezed her hand. "I'm glad you're here, Curlilocks."

Pink colored the edge of her smile. "There's nowhere I'd rather be than with you," she said.

The emotion shining in her eyes was more than he deserved. Unable to speak, he kissed her. Hard and greedily. "For luck," he whispered when they broke apart.

"O-okay." Her eyes were dazed, her lips swollen and glistening like the rain. A picture, he suspected, that would be in his head for a long while.

Slowly, his insides untwisted. They were here. No way would he turn back now. Planting one more kiss on her hand—for extra luck—he grabbed the door handle. "Come on, Curlilocks, let's go track down my son."

It took a lot of persuasion, as well as a donation to the new building fund, but Ian eventually walked out of the office armed with the information he needed.

"I don't think I want to know the amount on the check you wrote," Chloe said as they crossed the quad toward the building that housed Matt's last class.

"Money talks, Curli." A small price to pay as far as Ian was concerned. He'd paid far steeper sums for far less important things.

At least they were in between rainstorms. The morning's steady downpour had faded to a drizzle, meaning more students would be out and about.

Checking his watch, he saw it was five after the hour. "Class ended a few minutes ago. Why's he hanging around after?"

"Talking to friends, I bet. If he's done for the day, he's not in any rush."

"You're right." Ian couldn't let his impatience get the better of him. "I'm sure he…"

The doors to the building opened and a trio of students stepped outside. One look at the shock of auburn hair sticking out from beneath a baseball cap and Ian caught his breath.

He'd recognize the cocky strut anywhere. The determined shoulders. He was looking at a younger version of himself.

"Matt!" His voice rang out across the quad. The trio stopped, and so did he, a few feet shy of closing the gap. "Matt!" he called again, softer this time. The boy turned. It took a minute, but eventually his eyes widened in recognition. Ian raised a shaky hand. "Hey."

Silence filled the quad, stronger than before. "What are you doing here?" Matt finally asked.

"I came to see you," Ian replied. His heart permanently jammed itself in his throat. After all this time, they were finally speaking face-to-face. So many things he wanted to say. Where did he start?

"Did you get my messages?"

"I got them."

"Good. I didn't know if the storm—"

"If I wanted to talk, I would have called back."

What? Ian froze. "I don't understand. I thought we…" Words failed him. "We've been talking."

"I answered a couple letters. That doesn't mean I'm ready to get all buddy-buddy."

If he wanted you to know his phone number, wouldn't he have given it to you? Jack had said. Ian had screwed up. Again. He shoved the self-pity aside. This wasn't about him, it was about making things right with Matt. "I'm not looking to be your best friend. I understand I don't have that right."

"And yet you're here."

God, but the kid sounded so much like him it hurt. "If you'd give me five minutes—"

"No."

A slap would have hurt less.

"You need to hear your father out." It was Chloe. While he and Matt were talking, she'd stepped up to stand at his shoulder. Her fingers brushed the back of his hand, a featherlight gesture of support. It was all he could do not to grab hold.

Less appreciative of her presence, Matt stared her down. "Lady, I don't know who you are, but I don't need to do anything." He washed a hand over his features. "Look, I can't do this right now. I—I've got study group."

The worst thing about his son's rejection was Ian deserved every single bit. Mentally, he backed away, giving the kid the space he needed. "I'm sorry, Matt. I never meant to hurt you."

"If that's the case, then leave me alone. Find some other poor schmuck and call him. Just...ust..." He made the same face Ian made when searching for the right words. "Just back off."

"You want us to call security or something?" one of Matt's friends asked.

"Won't be necessary. Right?"

Ian nodded.

"You don't understand. Your father—"

"Let him go, Chloe." No need making things worse than he already had.

Incredulity filled her expression. "Are you nuts? You can't let him leave without explaining."

"Chloe—" Ian reached out to grab her arm, only to have her break free and jog after the trio.

"He's trying to make things right!" she called out to the kids. "Don't you understand what that's worth? How lucky you are?"

"I'm lucky?" Matt whirled around, his eyes hard as stone. "I don't know who you are, but that man did nothing for thirteen years. I'm not dropping everything because he decided to play father today. Now, leave me alone."

"But he—"

"Chloe, stop!"

Ian had had enough. Matt didn't want to listen. The only thing Chloe's pushing would do was drive the boy further away.

She refused to give up the fight, however. Her eyes had a desperate, manic shine to them as she gripped his arms. "Go after him," she demanded. "Tell him about all the events you attended. About graduation. He needs to know you were there."

"He doesn't want to hear it."

"Then make him! Follow him and make him listen."

"And how do you suggest I do that? Tackle him and hold him to the ground?" Didn't she realize he would if he thought forcing him would make a difference? Ian had messed up, pure and simple. What he needed to do was go home and regroup. Figure out how to fix what he'd destroyed.

He watched as Matt and his friends moved toward

another building. For one brief second, while standing in the doorway, it looked as though Matt glanced back in their direction, but he was merely holding the door open for someone else before vanishing behind the glass.

"Jack warned me. He said I should be more cautious."

But Ian hadn't listened, and as a result, he and his son might have had their one and only meeting. To think he might never hear Matt's voice again cut him in two. What had he done?

He never got the chance to apologize.

Chloe still wouldn't give up. She paced back and forth, her boots hitting the ground with hard steps. "You've got to go after him," she repeated. "We cannot come all this way, go through everything we went through, only to turn around. Tell me we aren't. That we aren't quitting."

"For crying out loud, Chloe, will you be quiet? We aren't doing anything." The words burst out of him like bullets, loud and fast. "This is about my son. You want to work out your father issues, do it on your own time."

She looked as if she'd been struck. "I can't believe you said that."

He could. He'd known it was only a matter of time before the monster inside him hurt her. This, he thought, as angry tears brightened her eyes, this was why he should have kept his distance.

The rain had returned. Chloe could feel the drops spitting in her face as she watched Ian walk away. With each step he took, the hope she dared to let hide in her chest grew fainter.

"You were supposed to be different," she whispered. Not like the others. He was supposed to stay and fight for the people he cared for. In her mind, the little girl she used to be gave up believing things could ever be different.

She found Ian in his car, staring at the steering wheel. "I told you I was a miserable bastard," he said.

"You had a rough day. It happens." The lame answer came from someplace she didn't recognize. Guess the hope hadn't completely died, as she was willing to forgive the outburst, even after he greeted her explanation with a humorless laugh.

"I should have listened to Jack."

"You said yourself some things can't be communicated in a letter."

"Because I know so much about parenting and relationships?"

"You weren't the only one who thought coming here was a good idea."

"Oh, I know."

He drawled the response, coating the words with bitterness. Chloe's hackles stood on edge. "What are you saying? You're not blaming me for this trip, are you?"

"Don't give yourself so much credit. You only confirmed what I wanted to hear."

Slowly, she pulled her scarf from around her neck. The wool was damp from the rain, but she spread the cloth over her legs, anyway. Kept her hands busy. "Nice to know I had such influence," she said, smoothing the plaid.

Ian replied with a long exhalation. "I'm sorry."

For what? Insulting her or bringing her along in the first place? There were so many ways she could take the comment. "I'm sure you are," she replied.

He jerked the shift stick out of position. "Might as well get going. We've got a long drive ahead of us."

An interminable drive at that. This time, however, it wasn't the weather, but the distance between driver and passenger making the trip uncomfortable. Ian didn't say a word and Chloe was too hurt, too frustrated, to try and draw him out. She spent the miles watching the rain streak her window.

The few times she looked in Ian's direction, her stomach churned into knots. His profile had turned so hard and reproachful, it hurt to look. Then there were her own insecurities. As much as she tried to tell herself it was the failed meeting with Matt causing his turmoil, she couldn't help worrying. If Ian could quit on the one person he claimed mattered more than anything in the world... With every mile that passed without contact or conversation, his angry words rang louder, and her insecurities grew stronger.

By the time they pulled up to the curb at her place, she was so tense she wanted to bolt straight from the car. "Home sweet home," she said softly, as much to the window as herself.

"Sorry I wasn't much company."

Said in the same terse voice he'd been using since leaving the university, the apology didn't hold much weight. He might as well have said "thanks for the good time" or "get out" for all the emotion behind his words.

Well, she'd be damned if she let her hurt feelings show. "Guess I'll see you at the coffee shop tomorrow."

"Sure." At last some emotion broke through. Unfortunately, that emotion was regret. Compounded by his finally reaching out to touch her. His hand gently cradled her cheek. "Good night, Curlilocks."

He meant goodbye. She saw the truth in his eyes. It took every effort, but she managed to step onto the sidewalk without showing her pain.

And to think this morning she'd actually almost thought about forever.

* * *

At least she could finally change her clothes and use her own hair dryer. Riding up in the elevator, she tried to list as many positives as possible. Anything to take her mind off the man who'd just driven away. She wouldn't have to sleep in Josef's nightshirt again, for example. One night was more than enough, thank you very much.

She much preferred sleeping in Ian's arms....

Stop being a crybaby. Ian had endured a devastating rejection. He had every right to be distant and preoccupied. Only a self-absorbed ninny would make this moment about her.

Except his kiss *did* feel like goodbye....

And what if it was? The elevator doors opened and she stepped onto her floor. Not the relationship type, remember? You both said so. Relationships were for people like Del and—

"Larissa?"

On the floor next to the door sat her best friend, knees pulled tight to her chest. As soon as Chloe said her name, she looked up with red-rimmed eyes. "I'm sorry I didn't call," she said. "I don't have my phone."

Her voice trembled as though she was barely holding it together. Chloe was frightened. "What happened? Are you okay?" A terrible thought occurred to her. "Is it Del—?"

Larissa shook her head. Fresh tears filled her eyes. "T-T-Tom left me."

What? "Oh, sweetie, no." She gathered the woman in her arms and hugged her tight.

Once Larissa calmed down a little, Chloe led her into her apartment and sat her on the love seat. La-roo immediately curled into the corner like a miserable blonde ball.

"I'm going to call Delilah," Chloe told her. This was

the kind of problem the three of them dealt with best together.

"No, don't," Larissa said. "This is her big week. I don't want to ruin it for her with my bad news."

"What happened? What do you mean, Tom left?" All Chloe could think was that Larissa misunderstood. Or she misunderstood Larissa.

"He said he met this woman at work, another broker, and they 'clicked'." She framed the word with her fingers. "Said she 'got him' better than I do. At least I think that's what he said. Honestly, I wasn't listening. I was too interested in getting out of the apartment."

"If that's the case, maybe you didn't hear the whole story," Chloe told her. That had to be it. "Maybe he had impure thoughts about this woman or something, and simply felt guilty. I bet if you call him—"

"He said 'I don't want to get married.' Not much there to misunderstand."

Dammit. Speechless, Chloe sank onto the sofa. Larissa was one of the good ones, too. Sweet, kind. Lovable. How could Tom walk out on her? What did that say about people like Chloe? "I don't understand," she murmured.

"I know. Everything was going so perfectly, too. We had the wedding all planned out.... "Oh my God, the wedding. What am I going to do about the wedding?" She burst into a fresh round of tears. "Why did this happen?"

Because men leave, Chloe thought as she rubbed her friend's back. No matter how wonderful they make you feel, they eventually walk away. The best thing you could do was to walk away first before they could cause too much damage.

CHAPTER TEN

"I KNEW YOU'D go off on your own the minute you hung up the telephone. Do you ever listen to advice?"

"You can skip the lecture, Jack. I already know I made a mistake." In more ways than one.

Squeezing his eyes shut, Ian massaged his temples, hoping the pressure would chase away the headache pounding in them. "I got impatient. You know as well as I do I suck at self-discipline."

He heard Jack let out a breath. "Self-discipline isn't your problem. It's stubbornness."

"You forgot selfishness," Ian added, raising his mug.

"Where are you now?"

"Where do you think? I needed solace, and I didn't want to go home." Another mistake, as things turned out. Opening his eyes, he looked around the vacant coffee shop. For the first time since buying the place, he found the atmosphere didn't bring comfort. Instead, the bright walls mocked him. Reminded him of firelight and spiral curls.

Amazing that it was Chloe he found himself thinking about. Matt was everything to him. His flesh and blood. The one real accomplishment in his life. Yet here he was, filled with as much self-loathing over hurting a girl—make that a woman—he'd known for less than a week as he was over hurting his son. How the hell did she get under his skin like that?

"See what I mean about self-discipline?" Jack was saying. "You could be in a bar."

"Doesn't mean I don't want to be. Only reason I'm not blitzed is I figured I'd screwed up enough this weekend."

Unfortunately, Jack could help him with only one of his mistakes. "I knew he was angry, but... I'd been so focused on apologizing." He'd never stopped to think about Matt's role in the equation. Ian had been selfish and stubborn as always.

Chloe's reaction had woken him up. He could still see her on the quad, desperate to make him to change his mind. And what did he do? Lose his temper. That's when it hit him. Time pulled back and he was once again hurting someone he cared about. Only this time he didn't have alcoholism to blame. Only himself.

"So what are you going to do?" Jack asked.

"Let her go."

"Don't you mean he?"

Right, they were talking about Matt. "What can I do? I can't walk away. I need to apologize."

"You did apologize, Ian. In your first letter, remember?"

Ian remembered. "I didn't tell him the whole truth, though. About the alcoholism, about watching him grow up." *He needs to know you didn't forget him.* Wasn't that what Chloe would say?

On the other end, Jack let out a long breath, a sign he was about to deliver a lecture. "Do you remember step nine?"

"You know I do." Make direct amends wherever possible. "I've been living the step for the past eighteen months."

"I know. Obsessively."

"What's that mean?"

Another long breath. "It means you don't have to be obsessive, Ian. 'Wherever possible.' Sometimes the best we can do is try."

"And if the attempt fails?"

"You live as good a life as you can and hope someday you get another chance."

"In other words, I can't make things happen on my timetable."

"I take it back, you did learn something."

Too little too late. Matt was furious with him, and Chloe...how the hell was he supposed to make amends to her? He wasn't sure he could be in the same room without wanting to pull her into his arms. Even tonight, frustrated and angry as he was, he longed to drive back to her apartment. So he could hold her again.

He must have sighed, because Jack asked, "What?"

"Nothing," he replied, then laughed. "Would you believe woman problems?"

"This the 'her' you're thinking of letting go?"

His sponsor was damn perceptive. "She's unlike any woman I've ever met, Jack. Sweet, innocent..." Vulnerable, kind.

"She sounds special."

"She is." Too special for the likes of him. A man whose entire legacy was causing pain to people he cared about.

"So what's the problem?"

"Nothing you can help with, unfortunately. This is one problem I have to solve myself." His eyes fell on the black garment bag lying on the counter.

He had one more amend to make. This one would be for her.

Having been up till five in the morning, Chloe did not appreciate hearing her apartment buzzer at nine-thirty. She rolled from bed, stole a glance at Larissa and headed into the living room. It was probably Delilah, worried over her two best friends calling in sick for work. "You could have phoned," she snapped into the speaker.

"I don't know your home number."

Ian? She was so surprised to hear his voice that for a second she forgot last night's resolve. "What are you doing here?"

"Can you let me in? We need to talk."

Actually, they didn't. Chloe was pretty certain their time for talking had ended when he'd kissed her goodbye last night. Anything Ian had to say now would only hurt.

But what if you're wrong?

The oath came out soft but sharp. *You're a glutton for punishment, Chloe Abrams.* "Fine." She unlatched the front door, then rushed to the bathroom to brush her teeth, purposely avoiding the mirror. She already knew she looked like a disaster; checking would only lead to panic. Instead, she grabbed a ponytail holder from the vanity drawer and shoved her curls atop her head. No sooner did she finish than Ian knocked.

It wasn't fair, an inner voice whined. Did he have to look so good? He wore his usual leather jacket and sweatshirt, with the familiar ginger shadow again covering his cheeks. Yesterday's sad, withdrawn expression remained as well, she noticed, only today a new emotion joined the mixture. Resignation. Defeat.

Disappointment settled in the pit of Chloe's stomach. She'd so hoped he might be different. She hated how he made her think that way.

At least now she knew the truth. His expression said everything she needed to know.

With a glance at the bedroom, she stepped out into the hall, closing the front door halfway. No need for Larissa to be dragged into the conversation. "What are you doing here?" she asked.

"When you didn't show up for your morning coffee I called your office, and they told me you phoned in sick. Are you all right?"

Wait a second. "You noticed I didn't come in for coffee?" He'd been looking for her.

Ian's response was to gaze at her as if she had two heads. "You've been coming in for thirty-two straight weeks. Of course I noticed you.

"You're a little hard to ignore," he added with a half smile.

Damn, but she hated how her heart fluttered when he gave his answer. Her heart had never fluttered until Ian. Further proof she'd made the right decision last night. Larissa's devastation was a harsh reminder of how important it was to protect your heart. For so long Chloe had told herself people got what they deserved. Until this weekend, when she'd let herself hope she might find forever. She'd been kidding herself. Ian was no different than any other man she'd let into her life.

With one exception: Ian had the power to break her heart if she let him get close.

"You didn't answer my question," he said. "Are you all right?"

"Fine." Man, but her face felt tight. She swore she wouldn't show emotion one way or another, but the action killed her check muscles. "Larissa got some bad news, and we spent the most of the night talking. I called in sick so we could get some sleep."

"I hope the news wasn't anything serious."

"Her fiancé broke up with her. He found someone else."

"I'm sorry."

There was sympathy in his eyes she didn't want to see, so she turned her attention to the weather-stripping on the side of her door. "Yeah, me, too. She deserved better."

"She wouldn't be the only one."

Chloe didn't want to discuss who deserved what; she simply wanted to get this conversation over with. The sooner she ripped the bandage off, the sooner the sting would start to heal. "Why are you here, Ian?" she asked. "Surely you didn't come by simply because I forgot my coffee."

"You left your dress in the backseat of the car."

For the first time she noticed the garment bag draped over his shoulder. "Figured you'd be looking for it come the end of the week," he said.

"Thanks." Gathering the bag in her arms, she held it tight, not caring if the dress wrinkled or not. Clutching helped her cope with the latest wave of disappointment. You'd think at some point she'd stop holding her breath for his response. "If that's everything…"

"I also wanted to talk."

And there it was; the true reason. He was going to stand in her hallway and tell her this weekend had been a mistake, or a one-time deal or, or, or…she knew a zillion excuses a man could give, and even if Ian did have the decency to deliver one of them to her face, she didn't want to hear it. Not from him. Not right now.

She started backing into her living room. "This isn't really a good time. What with La-roo being upset and everything."

"You said Larissa is asleep."

"Yeah, but…"

Ian reached around to pull her door shut. "This won't take long."

"Then why bother at all?"

He blinked. The question came out far sharper than Chloe meant it to. Usually she could fake indifference with the best of them. Thing was, she didn't feel indifferent this morning. Disappointed, agitated, but definitely not indifferent.

Taking a deep breath, she started again. "Look, what I'm saying is we both know the deal, so why go through the pretense? Why don't we save ourselves the hassle, agree that this weekend was fun while it lasted, and move on?"

"Do you really mean that?" Ian moved so that he shared the door frame with her, his broad chest consuming what little space her own body didn't. When he folded his arms across his torso, the action brought him right up against her. With a narrowed gaze, he looked her in the eye. The intensity made Chloe want to squirm. She missed her high heels and the height advantage they gave her. They were eye to eye right now, and she'd never felt more pinned down in her life.

"Sure," she said, finding her voice. "Don't you? I mean, isn't that why you're here? To end things on a nice clean note?"

It was his turn to squirm. She'd made up her mind last night that this time she would walk away first. "Some people aren't cut out for relationships, right? Wasn't that what you said?"

"I wasn't talking about you. You're—"

"No." He did not get to play the martyr and feel better about himself. "I'm the same as you, Ian."

"That's where you're wrong." Before she knew what happened, his fingers were playing with the loose curls by her face. "You, Curlilocks—"

"Stop calling me that!" Her frustration boiled over and she slapped his hand away. Forget indifferent. "You do not tell me what I am and what I'm not. I'm the one standing in my hallway in a pair of ratty yoga pants being tossed aside, so I get to be the one to walk away. Me, not you. And if that leaves you feeling bad or guilty or un-lovable, then tough. Deal with it."

Her vision started to blur. Dammit, she would not lose control more than she already had. She reached for the door handle, only for Ian to catch her by the wrist.

"You are not unlovable," he whispered.

Of everything she'd said, why on earth did he pick that word to zero in on? Keeping her jaw clenched, she stared straight ahead. "Hey, we all get what we deserve, right?"

His stuttered breath gave her a small measure of sat-isfaction. "I never meant..."

"Cross my name off your list, Ian. You've made all the amends here you're going to make."

Breaking free, she finally managed to open her door and get herself inside. Ian didn't stop her.

Did you expect he would? Chloe let her head fall back against the door. Walking away wasn't any better than being brushed off.

"Did I hear the door?" Larissa asked, stepping out of the bedroom. Her face still bore mascara traces from last night's cryfest.

Chloe quickly mustered a smile. "I left my dress in the backseat of Ian's car. He stopped by to return it."

"I thought it might be Tom."

"Sorry." Based on everything she'd heard last night, Tom wouldn't be stopping by in the near future.

Larissa shrugged and shuffled toward the kitchen. "This is Ian from the coffee shop, right? The rich slacker?"

"One and the same," Chloe replied.

"I thought you said you weren't interested. How'd you end up going away with him for the weekend?"

"Long story." A long, depressing story, and La-roo had enough on her plate to deal with. Opening the fridge, Chloe searched for the orange juice. "You don't want to know."

"Come on; tell me. I need to talk about something other than my problems. What happened?"

Chloe told her the bare-bones story.

"Wow. Stranded at a mountain inn. That sounds so romantic."

"Only because you're addicted to romance," she replied, handing her a glass of juice. Even as she protested, however, scenes from the weekend laid themselves out in her head.

"Maybe, but you're not nearly as unaffected by it as you pretend to be," Larissa retorted. "You cannot tell me you spent the entire weekend under those conditions and didn't feel even a little spark."

Chloe's heated skin betrayed her. She tried to hide behind her orange juice, and failed.

"Oh my God, you did!" Chloe's skin burned hotter. "That's wonderful! Makes me glad to know both my friends have decent love lives."

That was Chloe's line. "Better change the number to one."

"I thought you said you and Ian...?"

"We did, but it was only a weekend fling."

"Why?"

"Because." Because she wasn't worth more. "You know I'm not interested in a relationship. That's yours and Del's thing."

"I'm doing real well in that department, aren't I?"

Seeing the dejection on Larissa's face made Chloe's

already beat-up emotions feel worse. "I'm sorry, La-roo. I didn't mean to be insensitive."

"You weren't. My new single status is something we both need to get used to. But I also don't believe you. You may say you don't want a relationship, but I don't buy it for a minute."

"Don't be ridiculous." The conversation was getting uncomfortable. "Do you want me to make breakfast or do you want to head to the diner corner?"

"I'm not hungry. Do you want to know why I don't believe you?"

"Because analyzing me will cheer you up?"

The blonde shook her head. "Because you make the same speech every time you end a relationship. You make a very big point of stating how you weren't emotionally invested."

"Because I usually wasn't," Chloe reminded her.

"Methinks the lady protests too much."

Seriously? She was going to psychoanalyze, and quote Shakespeare? "I need coffee if you're going to do this," Chloe muttered.

She reached for the coffee pods, grabbed one and dropped it into the brewing chamber. "And for the record, I do not protest too much. Some people simply aren't meant to find love. I'm one of them."

For a moment, the only sound in the kitchen was that of the coffee streaming into her mug.

"Why on earth would you think you aren't meant to find love?" Larissa asked after a moment. Did Chloe really say that out loud? Damn.

"I meant be loved. Be in love."

"Use whatever phrase you want, it's still not true. You're as worthy as anyone."

"Have you checked my dating record?" She tried to sound flippant, but the attempt sounded flat.

"No offense, Chloe, but that's because you tend to date losers."

Maybe you need to date a better class of guy. Ian's words repeated in her ear.

"I thought this time I was."

"What?"

Seeing the confused look on Larissa's face, she realized she'd spoken out loud. "I thought this time was different."

"You mean Ian."

Chloe nodded. "But he walked away, too. Or he was about to."

"What do you mean, 'about to'?"

"I beat him to the punch."

Larissa's jaw dropped. "You broke up with him? Chloe, what were you thinking? You don't know if he was planning to walk away."

"Yes," she said, "I do."

"How?"

"Because I've been dumped enough times to know the signs, that's how!"

She shouldn't have shouted, but arguing the point made the wound raw again. Larissa didn't taste the goodbye in his kiss or see the regret in his expression.

"He told me I deserved better," she said in a softer voice. "All I did was preempt the inevitable."

Tears threatened to burn her eyes. Refusing to give them a chance, she slid to the floor. Drawing her legs tight against her, she let her forehead fall to her knees. The same pose she'd found Larissa in last night.

"Oh, Chloe." A warm presence materialized on the

floor next to her, followed by an arm around her shoulders. "He's a jerk. Tom's a jerk. All men are jerks."

"I'll give you Tom, but Ian?" She shook her head. Much as it hurt, she couldn't call him a bad name. "He was nothing but honest from the start." If anything, she was the one who wasn't special enough to change his mind.

"You really like him, don't you?"

"Yeah," she whispered into her knees. At last she admitted the truth she'd been fighting since Friday night. "I like him a lot." More than liked, actually. Somehow he'd gotten past all her defenses and captured the very thing she swore she'd never risk. Her heart.

No wonder breathing hurt.

"At least Delilah found Simon, and those two are definitely soul mates," Larissa was saying. Good old La-roo, looking for the silver lining. "So they do exist. We'll have to wait a little longer to find ours, is all."

Chloe bit back her discouraged reply. No doubt Larissa would bounce back and find true love, but her?

She couldn't help but believe her soul mate had kissed her goodbye last night.

Given how she felt, only an idiot would go to the coffee shop the next morning.

"We could go to the place across the street," said Larissa, who met her on the corner.

Chloe didn't want to go to the place across the street. "Absolutely not. Do you plan to stop eating dinner at the pub?" she asked, referring to the little restaurant where Larissa and Tom used to grab dinner.

"No, but that's different. The pub is in my neighborhood. I was meeting you guys there before Tom and I met."

"This is the same thing. I've been visiting this coffee

shop for months. I didn't stop coming after Aiden, and I refuse to stop coming now." It was a matter of pride.

Plus, possibly, she wanted to make a point of showing Ian what he'd given up. She'd taken extra care with her appearance, going for a leather jacket and dangerously high heels, the kind that turned heads on the subway. The cut on her chin was almost healed and she'd done her makeup to perfection. The only way anyone would know she wasn't 100 percent together was if she removed her sunglasses and revealed the circles underneath her eyes. Vestiges of another lousy night's sleep. She didn't plan on removing the glasses. Not in front of Ian.

Forcing her head high, she strutted down the sidewalk with such long strides Larissa had to double-time to keep up. "What are you going to do if he wants to talk?" the blonde asked when they were four doors down.

"I'm not. We said everything yesterday." And she wasn't ready for friendly small talk.

No more banter, she realized. The back-and-forth might have lasted only a week, but she couldn't picture being in the shop without Ian's sandpapery voice teasing her about something. She'd miss talking most of all. The sense of connection that had them finishing each other's sentences, as though they were two halves of the same brain.

Great. Two doors away and she was already getting emotional. Maybe she should have gone to the other place, after all. Blinking away the moisture, she adjusted her sunglasses and pulled open the front door.

Ian's absence was the first thing either of them noticed. "I thought you said he hung out at the front table?" Larissa remarked.

"He usually does." The table sat empty today. "Must be out back."

Her sixth sense said otherwise, though. There was a noticeable chill in the air that wasn't normally present, while the red and orange walls—which she'd told him inspired warmth—looked garish. Even the furniture possessed a worn indifference. They were missing the ingredient that brought them to life.

As if fate wanted to truly hammer home a message, Aiden waited on them. "Ian's not here," he said. "He said something about having to take off for a few days."

"See?" Chloe said when the barista turned around. "Told you he wouldn't want to talk with me."

She couldn't have felt worse if she tried.

CHAPTER ELEVEN

For the amount of money he'd donated the past two days, you'd think he could get a decent cup of coffee. Obviously, the university president didn't appreciate flavor as much as he appreciated signed checks. Then again, beggars couldn't be choosers. The man was already treading a thin ethical line by doing him this favor. Ian set his half-empty cup on the desk and resumed his pacing. Every so often his eyes would stray to the clock on the wall. Checking the time. Wouldn't be long now.

He'd made the drive in record time. Motor across a state three or four times in as many days and you got used to the route. He'd done this trip in one straight shot, no stops.

Although he did slow down when he passed the exit for the Bluebird.

Ian rubbed the center of his chest. Damn heartburn had bothered him since leavng the city. Simultaneously sharp and throbbing, the pain felt as if something had smashed a giant hole in his sternum.

Make that someone. The hole had formed the second Chloe closed the door in his face.

If only she knew how badly he'd wanted to bang on that door, drag her back into the hallway and kiss her senseless. Thankfully, he'd kept his impulse reined in.

He'd done the right thing, walking away. Sure, she hurt now. That so-called casual attitude didn't fool him for a bit—even before the meltdown. In time, however—in the long run—she would be better off. She'd find a great guy, fall in love, and make his mornings better by being there when he opened his eyes.

Ian rubbed his sternum again.

We get what we deserve. Her parting words, and his wish for her. If that meant he had to deal with heartburn for the rest of his life, then so be it.

The door opened, stopping him in his tracks. "I got a message to come see you— Crap, you don't give up, do you?"

"Not when it matters," Ian replied. Crossing the room in two strides, he reached over the teenager's head to shut the door. "I'm not letting you walk away this time."

"Seriously? You're not letting me walk away."

Ian winced. The kid wasn't making things easy, but Ian held his ground. Today's visit wasn't about him. He was here to set Matt free, and for Chloe. So she'd know he cared enough to fight. "Five minutes. And when I'm done, you never have to speak with me again."

Matt stared at the oak door. The kid was wavering. Otherwise, he would have walked out by now. "How much did it cost you to get Dean Zobreist to do your dirty work?" he asked.

"You don't want to know."

"I hope you get your money's worth."

"I already have. You're still here."

"Okay." He turned around and folded his arms across his chest. "Five minutes," he repeated, chin jutting forward. "Four minutes and thirty seconds actually."

Talk about a chip off the old block. Ian took a deep breath. "I was wrong to surprise you the other day. I—I wanted us to reconnect so badly, I didn't stop to think about how you might feel."

"So you decided to surprise me again to apologize."

There was a certain irony to the arrangement, wasn't there? "Not to apologize. To give you this." Reaching into his breast pocket, he pulled out a letter. His final letter of amends. "This explains everything that happened over the last thirteen years. When you're ready, I hope you'll read it. After, if you want to talk, you call me. I'll meet you whenever and wherever. You call the shots."

Matt stared at the envelope. "That's it?"

"Unless you want to talk now."

"I'm not—"

"Ready. I know." Ian stepped away from the door. Matt immediately reached for the handle. "I love you very much, Matt. I always have."

"You have a funny way of showing it," his son replied.

"Love isn't always visible. Someday I hope you'll realize that my being around would have only made things worse for you."

The teenager started through the door, only to stop and turn around. "I believe you, you know," he said, the words going straight to Ian's heart. "But it would have been nice if I'd had a choice."

He was getting one now. For the third time in three days, Ian let someone he cared about walk away, and it ripped his insides in two.

He waited until he was back in his car before calling Jack.

"How'd it go?" the lawyer asked.

"About as well as could be expected. At least he didn't throw the envelope in my face."

"Good news there. Who knows? Maybe the kid'll come around someday."

"Maybe," Ian replied. Although he didn't think he'd hold his breath, waiting for the moment. There were many layers of resentment and disappointment to be worked through even if Matt did read his apology. Could scars like that ever truly be healed?

Ian thought of Chloe, who was still hoping for an explanation from her own father, and wondered. Wondered if the man ever sat in his car kicking himself for ignoring such a beautiful, unique, amazing woman. If so, Ian hoped the guy felt as guilt-ridden as he did.

He let his head fall back against the headrest. "Do you think I was right to keep my distance all those years?"

"Between the alcohol and the Jeanine factor, you can certainly put forth a good argument. Why?"

"Just wondering. Matt said something on the way out the door. Made me wonder how bad the damage would have been had I stayed in touch."

"I'm going to guess there would be damage caused either way. You were a bastard until you got sober, or did you forget?"

"How could I when I've got you to remind me?"

"True." There was a brief silence on the other end. Ian could picture the lawyer grinning. "What exactly did he say, anyway?"

"He accused me of not giving him a choice."

"Of course you didn't. He was five years old and you were…"

"A drunk, I know." Chances were, if he'd stayed, he would have inflicted the same damage on Matt that his father had inflicted on him.

"Either way," Jack continued, "there's little you can do about your decision now. What's done is done. Best you can do, if you did make a mistake, is try to fix things, and hope you don't make the same mistake again."

The thing was, had he learned? All the way back to the city, Ian couldn't shake the notion that he'd forgotten a piece of the lesson.

Matt's comment kept ringing in his head: *I didn't have a choice.* Jack was right, of course. The kid had been five years old at the time. Ian walked away to protect an innocent boy. He couldn't offer Matt a choice. Maybe, if he'd been an adult...

You mean like Chloe?

Crap. Ian practically slammed on the brakes, the thought reared up on him so abruptly. What did Chloe have to do with all this?

A stupid question. She and Matt had been twisted together for days now. Think of Matt's abandonment and Chloe's story wasn't far behind. Picture Matt's angry face and Chloe's disappointed expression followed. Hell, think of anything and thoughts of Chloe tagged along. In a few short days, she'd managed to permanently attach herself to his brain. More than his brain, he amended, rubbing at the hole in his chest.

The more he thought about it, given their shared childhood experiences, the commonalities between Matt and Chloe didn't surprise him. Ian wondered if his son faced the world with the same edge and bravado. The first day she'd strutted her way into his coffee shop...man, but she'd looked so sassy. He realized now she wore her attitude like a shield. All her talk about not being the relationship type? Her way of getting out in front of any hurt the world might deal her.

It's what she'd been doing yesterday morning, too. He could tell because her eyes had the desperate sheen to them that came from trying too hard.

But when she dropped her defenses... Then those eyes grew so soft and vulnerable, a man could drown in them.

Ian could see her now. Eyes brimming with emotion in the firelight. She'd given him a gift, he realized. A window into a part of her she didn't share with too many people. That glimpse stole his heart.

Who was he kidding? She'd stolen his heart the moment she gave Aiden a peppermint latte shower. All Saturday night did was cement her hold on Ian.

But he'd pushed her way. Just like with Matt, he'd pulled back because he'd decided distance was for the best. He took away her choice.

"Idiot." Ian added a few other choice adjectives as well while pounding the steering wheel. All his talk about no longer being selfish, and here he was, being as selfish as ever.

How many losses would he have to endure before the lesson kicked in? His son, his company, years of sobriety—all lost because of his stubbornness. His insistence on doing things his way. And now here he was, insisting he knew best again. He'd already lost Matthew. Did Ian want to be sitting in his car twenty years from now, mourning Chloe, too? Because Lord knows, he wouldn't find another woman like her again. She was one of a kind.

The car behind blared its horn, then passed him on the right, the driver offering up an obscene gesture on the way by. Ian started to glare in return until he glanced at the speedometer and saw he'd slowed down to thirty miles an hour. He needed to get his mind off Chloe before he caused an accident.

Would if it were that easy, he said to himself as he pulled over a lane. The upcoming exit sign caught his eye and he gasped. Looked like the universe was full of messages today, wasn't it? Flipping on his direction signal, he eased right again and prepared to turn off the highway. Same exit he and Chloe had taken leaving the Bluebird. With luck Josef and Dagmar would have a room he could use for a few days. He had a lot of thinking to do.

"They look great together, don't they?" Larissa asked with a sigh. "So much in love."

So much in love it hurt, thought Chloe. She licked the cinnamon from the rim of her appletini and watched Delilah get twirled around the dance floor by her new husband. Their friend had two left feet. Every so often she would trip over her partner, the stumble sending both of them into giggles and kisses. They were perfect for one another.

They danced in the center of a lantern-lit floor. The Landmark Hotel ballroom had been bathed in white satin for the evening, the only color being the blue of the centerpiece flowers, which coordinated with the attendants' dresses. Beautiful and perfectly matched. Like the couple on the dance floor.

One of the groomsmen approached the table. "Would one of you ladies like to dance?" he asked. Chloe sipped her drink and pretended not to hear him, leaving Larissa to smile and take his hand. Not, however, before shooting a quick glare in her direction.

She should probably feel bad about throwing La-roo under the bus, but honestly, she didn't think her friend truly minded, and even if she did, she would still make a far better dance partner. While she might be heartbroken, Larissa still loved weddings, and was pouring her all into enjoying this one. Chloe, on the other hand, had all she could do to keep a smile on her face. It wasn't that she didn't wish her friends every happiness in the world. She did. It was that every time she looked at Simon and Delilah, she saw a happiness she'd never have. Seeing them was like sticking a knife in her heart.

Nearly five days had passed since she'd closed the door on Ian. Four days since she'd seen his face, heard his raspy voice. The sucker in her insisted on visiting the coffee shop every morning, looking for his ginger-scruffed face sitting at the front table, only to be disappointed. According to Aiden, Ian hadn't returned from his "getaway." She wondered if he wasn't simply avoiding her.

Shouldn't the pain hurt less by now? She licked more cinnamon and wondered. Granted, this level of heartache was new, but she hoped she'd be feeling better. That the emotions ripping her apart every time she thought of his name would begin to fade. No such luck. It appeared that when Ian went, he'd left behind a giant hole too big for filling.

"Why aren't you dancing? You should be dancing." A giddy Delilah, her eyes glittering manically, plopped down at the table. "That dress looks way too stunning to be stuck behind a table."

"Larissa's showing the dress off for us both," Chloe replied. "I need to stay on alert in case important maid of honor business comes up." It was the same excuse she'd been using for two days to avoid socializing.

Apparently Delilah had figured out her plan, because she waved off the excuse. "Your duties are officially over. I'm Simon's problem now. Wait, that didn't come out right."

"How much champagne have you had to drink?"

"Not as much as you'd think. I'm simply really, really, really happy." As if Chloe couldn't tell. Delilah's face glowed so brightly she could power Manhattan and half of Brooklyn, too.

"I'm glad," she replied, meaning it sincerely. "You deserve happiness."

"Thanks. I can't help feeling a little guilty, though, what with you and Larissa having such rotten weeks."

"Don't you dare! No guilt allowed on your wedding day, Mrs. Cartwright. Larissa and I will be fine." Chloe looked over at her fellow bridesmaid, who was chatting away with her dance partner. "In fact, I think La-roo will bounce back quite nicely."

"What about you?"

She managed a smile for Delilah's sake. "I'll bounce back, too." Eventually. She was nothing if not resilient.

"I hope so," Delilah replied. Before Chloe could say another word, she gathered her in a tight hug. Wrapped tight, Chloe allowed the emotion to bubble to the surface. She squeezed her eyes and her friend.

"For the record," Delilah whispered in her ear. "Ian Black's an ass."

Chloe sniffed back her tears. "Yes," she said, "he is."

The moment was interrupted by the band leader speaking into the microphone. "May I have your attention, please. It's time for the bride to toss the bouquet."

"Oh man," Chloe groaned. "I thought you decided not to."

"Larissa insisted."

Of course she did. With luck her friend would catch the foolish thing, too. Chloe sat back to sip her drink.

"What do you think you're doing?" Delilah took the glass from her hand. "As maid of honor you're required to be on the dance floor."

"You said my duties were over!"

"I lied."

Standing on a dance floor fighting over who caught a bunch of flowers was the last thing she felt like doing, but since Delilah and Larissa had their hearts set on it, she would go join the crowd. Someone else could do the catching, though, she decided, grabbing her drink. She made her way to the back of the area while a beaming Simon led his bride to the stage. Delilah grinned at the crowd, turned her back and tossed the flowers high. Too high, it turned out. The bouquet struck the chandelier and ricocheted straight down, landing at Chloe's feet.

A tuxedo-clad arm reached down to retrieve the fallen blossoms. "What's the matter, Curlilocks? Rebounding a little rusty?"

Silk over sandpaper ran down her spine, stilling her heart. Slowly she turned. This couldn't be real. Ian was not standing there clutching a bunch of limp flowers.

He offered the bouquet with a cautious smile. "Thought maybe you could use a dance partner."

She tossed the appletini in his face.

"Are you nuts?" Larissa and Delilah had cornered her in the ladies' lounge.

"Three days!" she snapped at them. "Tells me I deserve better and then takes off for three solid days. Do you have any idea how miserable I was? Now he shows up acting like nothing ever happened. What did he think I would do—throw myself in his arms? Who does he think he is?"

She pressed her hands to the marble vanity, hoping the coolness beneath her palms would help sort the feelings swirling inside her. "What is he doing here?"

"My guess would be he's here to see you," Delilah replied.

"In a tuxedo," Larissa added.

"Don't go there." Chloe should have known the blonde would find Ian's appearance romantic. "Every man in the room is wearing one."

"Every man in the room didn't crash the wedding,"

she shot back. "He came to see you. Maybe he wants to try again."

For how long? Until she got her hopes high enough for him to dash again? "And what if I don't want to?"

"What are you talking about?" Larissa's reflection stared at her in disbelief. "You're crazy about him. You told me so yourself."

Maybe so, but she wasn't crazy enough to have her heart stomped on a second time. She wouldn't survive. "He should have acted while he had the chance. I don't think I'm interested anymore."

"That's a crock and you know it. You've been going to that damn coffee shop twice a day, hoping to see him. Now he shows up and you say you're not interested? Pulleeze. I'm blonde, not stupid."

"All right, fine!" Chloe should have known her indifference act wouldn't work. "So I'm crazy about him. How do I know he's going to stick around this time? That he isn't going to make a whole bunch of promises and take off? Face it," she said, staring down at the marble. "Men suck."

"Not every guy leaves," Larissa said.

"Tom did."

"Simon didn't." Delilah appeared next to her. "Do you remember before Simon and I got engaged? When we were having problems, and the two of you helped him track me down to talk?"

"Of course I remember. But you and Simon were a completely different situation. The two of you were miserable without each other."

"And you've been miserable all week."

"Look," Larissa said, "no one is saying you have to give Ian any kind of chance. He broke your heart, and if you want to kick him to the curb, then we'll help. Before you do, though, aren't you the least bit curious to know why he tracked you down?"

Chloe had to admit she was. Her friends had a point. She should hear him out. If for no other reason than to keep her hopes at bay. Then she'd kick him to the curb.

"He's right outside, waiting," Delilah told her. "He wanted to come in and corner you himself, but we convinced him it would be safer if we did."

With her heart stuck somewhere between her chest and her throat, Chloe opened the lounge door. Ian stood across the corridor, wiping the front of his shirt with a napkin. "I forgot how lethal you were with a glass of liquid," he remarked when he saw her.

"You caught me by surprise."

"Clearly."

No wonder Larissa had pointed out the tuxedo. Ian might be dressed like the other guests, but none of them wore the suit nearly as well.

"They told me at the coffee shop you were out of town?" Not the question she'd planned to ask, but the first one to pop out of her mouth nonetheless.

"I went back to Pennsylvania."

"To see Matt again?" Did that mean Ian hadn't given up on his son, after all?

That still didn't mean anything had changed between the two of *them,* she reminded herself when hope threatened to blossom. Matt was his flesh and blood.

"I decided to change tactics. One of the things we learn in rehab is amends aren't about you. They are about making things right for the other person. I was so focused on completing my plan, I forgot."

"How'd it go?"

"Verdict's still out."

Chloe nodded. No matter what happened between her and Ian, she hoped he made peace with his son.

She stared at the man who'd upended her world. Too shocked by his arrival to notice before, she realized now how tired he looked. Tense, too. Reminded her very much of Saturday afternoon, when he'd been so stressed over meeting his son. "Why are you here?" she finally asked.

"Isn't it obvious?"

"Frankly, no. I thought we said everything Tuesday morning."

Ian crumpled in his fist the napkin he'd been holding. "I made a huge mistake that morning," he said.

"Look, if this is another amends mission, I already told you you're off the hook."

"Not this time."

Chloe sighed. She hurt too much to assuage his guilt. "Well, then I guess you'll have to deal."

"Chloe, please wait." She'd turned to leave, only to have him catch her hand. A week didn't diminish the effect of his touch. Every inch of her skin tingled with memory. "I need to say this," he told her. "Give me five minutes. Then, if you want me to go, I will."

CHAPTER TWELVE

FIVE MINUTES. SAME request he'd asked of his son. Pulling her hand away, she tried to still the tingling by squeezing her shoulder. "Five minutes," she repeated. Then she was out of there.

"My whole life I did things on my terms. The way I built my company, the way I dealt with my demons. The way I raised my son."

"You're eating up your time," Chloe said. "I know all this."

"Point is, because I was rich and successful, I figured I had all the answers. That I knew best. That included measuring my mistakes. Because I thought Matt was better off without me, there could be no other solution. The kid never had a choice. I did the same thing with you. I decided I wasn't good enough for you, so I decided to pull away.

"Only you beat me to the punch," he added.

Chloe, however, was stuck on something he'd said earlier. Not good enough for her? Seriously? "So, what, you're back because you've decided you are good enough for me?"

Ian stopped pacing. "No." Chloe's heart sank.

"Do you have any idea how amazing and special you

are?" he went on. "I don't think I'll ever be good enough. Not in a million years."

Perfect words, but could she believe him? "Words are cheap."

"You're right, they are. I wish I knew an answer to make you believe what I'm saying, but I can't. I'm learning love doesn't come with guarantees."

If only it— *"Love?"* The word hung between them, waiting to be claimed.

He looked down at his hands, a frustrating move because it meant she couldn't see his face. After using the word, she needed to read his eyes.

"After I left Matt the other day, my mind wouldn't stop spinning. I needed a place to think."

It wasn't the direction Chloe expected their conversation to travel. With her nails digging into the palms of her hand to keep her body from trembling, she waited for him to make his point.

"I went back to the Bluebird," he told her. That was a surprise.

"You wouldn't leave my head. One minute I'm driving, thinking about you, the next I'm staring at the exit. I took it as a sign that that's where I needed to go.

"I spent the past couple days in the room we shared, trying to pinpoint what made our time together so incredibly right. When I wasn't in the room, I was talking to Josef and Dagmar. They gave me some pretty sound advice. Did you know they've been married thirty-five years?"

"That's very sweet, but at the moment I don't care." Chloe's nails were carving permanent lines in her skin. This journey of self-discovery was all well and good, but he'd mentioned love. She needed to know what he meant.

"Ah, my sweet little Curlilocks, I love how impatient you are."

There he went again, throwing the word *love* around. Each time, her breath would catch, as she waited for the reality check. "Ian, please, what are you trying to tell me?"

"I'm saying I've got a lot of baggage."

Reality struck. The damn baggage again. She should have known.

She turned to leave.

"But..." His voice stopped her. "But," he continued, sounding a step closer than before, "sitting in that room surrounded by thoughts of you, it dawned on me that so does everyone else in this world. It's what we do with that baggage that counts. Look past, move forward."

"I don't understand." Actually, she was afraid to try. His words sounded too good, made her heart too hopeful. It was getting harder and harder to keep her feelings reined in. If she let herself believe and she was wrong...

The hands that suddenly caressed her shoulders didn't help. "All this time I've been focused on earning people's forgiveness," he said. "Turns out there was one very important person who never made the list."

"Who's that?"

"Me. I ignored one of the most important lessons of all—to forgive myself for my mistakes. Matt, the drinking, the pigheadedness. Of course, when you stop to think, it makes sense. I was being pigheaded about forgiveness."

Despite her churning nerves, she had to smile at the irony. "Sounds like a great epiphany."

"And it's all because of you."

Her? She turned to see his face. The sincerity in his expression shocked her. "What did I do?"

"Walked into my life," Ian replied as he swiped a thumb across her cheek. Almost as if brushing away a tear. Blinking, she realized that's exactly what had happened. She'd been so busy reining in her heart, she didn't register the emotion wetting her eyes.

"One of the reasons I was so intent on fixing the past was because it was all I had. Other than the coffee shop, I didn't have a future. At least I didn't until a gorgeous, curly-haired drink-tosser walked into my store. I couldn't resist you."

He'd said the same words in Pennsylvania, only with far less devotion. "You called it your weakness on Saturday night," she reminded him.

"You're right, I did say that. Because I was too blind and stubborn to see I was weak for a reason. That I'm completely and utterly nuts about you."

He cradled his face in his palms and stared into her eyes, the posture so much like their first kiss she nearly fell into his arms then and there. Not yet, though. All his sweet talk was wonderful, but the fact remained, he'd cast her aside once. He could do so again. Her fear must have crossed her face, because there was his thumb brushing her cheek again. "I know I hurt you, Chloe. In my mind, I thought I was doing the right thing by walking away, but in reality, I was only dooming us both to being miserable. Truth is, I love you, Chloe Abrams."

Her heart stopped. "You—you love me?"

"With all my heart, and I want nothing more than to spend my days and nights showing you how much."

"I don't know...." Breaking away, she stumbled toward a nearby credenza. *You idiot*, her insides screamed. *Ian Black just said he loved you.* Her heart had recovered and was pumping with joy, the beats so loud everyone in the hotel could hear.

Fear, however, refused to let up its grip. Say she gave in, admitted she was as much in love with him. What would happen a week from now? Two? What if he decided his baggage was too much to handle, after all, and left? "I'm not sure I could handle another rejection," she murmured.

"I know. Which is why I'm not going to pressure you. It's an amazing rarity, in that I actually learned a second lesson this weekend. Forgiveness doesn't come on my schedule. That's why, as crazy as I am about you, I won't force you to decide anything today."

The hands returned to her shoulders, this time gently turning her around. His eyes were as dark and passionate as Chloe had ever seen. "I'm not walking away," he told her. "I'm waiting for you. And I'll wait as long as it takes"

His kiss was tender. Sweet without pressing, and so full of love, Chloe ached. Needing purchase, lest she fall, she grabbed his forearms. When the kiss finally ended, she kept her grip. Ian was her stability.

"See you soon, I hope, Curlilocks," he whispered. Pressing one last kiss to her forehead, he started to walk away.

Chloe clutched at her middle. *Run after him*, her heart screamed. Not only did he claim to love her, he'd said he would wait until she made up her mind. No man had ever done that. Forget being rejected. Ian was right, love didn't come with guarantees.

Her feet still wouldn't move. She was still too scared.

A flash of white distracted her. From the corner of her eye she saw Simon grabbing Delilah's arm to prevent her from coming over. He whispered something in his bride's ear, and kissed her cheek. The softness in his expression took Chloe's breath away. She'd seen the exact same expression on Ian's face when he'd kissed her.

What kind of idiot walked away from such a gift? Ian was offering her the opportunity to be loved, as well as the choice to walk away. Knowing his need to be in charge, she sensed the call to hold back had to be murder.

She might love him more for that sacrifice alone.

"Ian, wait!" The bouquet lay on the credenza where he'd left it. She grabbed the flowers and heaved them across the hall. Ian caught them the second he turned around.

"You know what it means when you catch the bridal bouquet right?" she said, rushing up to him.

The adoring expression returned to his face, filling her heart and making her realize she'd made the right choice. Her. Chloe Abrams, who was never destined for love, had finally picked the right guy. "It means the maid of honor falls in love with you."

She gasped as Ian pulled her close. "If that means getting you, I'll catch a thousand bouquets."

"You only need one." Hoping her eyes reflected the love he'd unlocked, she shoved her fear aside and kissed him.

Five weeks later, spring finally and permanently arrived in New York. With the arm of the man she loved draped around her shoulders, Chloe let the sun warm her skin. "Today is the perfect day," she said to Ian. "I can't believe Larissa would rather be in Mexico."

"Personally, I'm having a harder time believing she went on her destination wedding alone."

They were walking back to the coffee shop after seeing Larissa off at her apartment. The blonde had surprised everyone last week by announcing she planned to keep her hotel reservations, and go on her honeymoon. "I spent a year of my life planning this trip, practically down to the shells on the beach," she told them. "I am going regardless."

"I've got to give her credit. She seems to be handling the breakup with Tom a lot better than I thought. In fact, I think she was more emotional about having to give up the wedding."

Ian pressed a kiss to Chloe's temple. "I've been thinking, when we get married, we should have a destination wedding, too."

"Yeah?" A thrill passed through her when he said the word. Ian spent a lot of time mentioning weddings and their future. Most of the references she believed were to ease her fears, thinking that the more he talked about forever, the more she would believe he planned to stay. Thus far, the tactic was working. Every day that she woke up and saw his face on the pillow next to her, or heard his voice on the telephone, she grew more and more convinced she'd found a love to last a lifetime. "Where were you thinking we should go? Mexico?"

"Pennsylvania. We could go back to the Bluebird Inn and celebrate where we began."

Chloe couldn't think of anything she'd love more. "Why wait for a wedding?" she said, snuggling closer. "I bet the inn is beautiful this time of year."

"I like how you think." He stopped to give her a lingering kiss.

"Um, hi."

She felt Ian stiffen as soon as he heard the greeting. He reached for her hand as Matt pushed away from the coffee shop door to walk toward them. The youth stopped a couple feet away. Hands shoved in his back pockets, he scuffed his running shoe back and forth across the sidewalk. "Did you really attend my graduation?" he asked finally.

He'd read Ian's letter. Thank heavens. As good as things were between her and Ian, she knew the loss of his son ate away at him. Keeping his promise to give Matt space hadn't been easy, but he'd kept his word.

"I went to a lot of things," Ian told him. Both spoke softly, as if worried that a raised voice would make the other bolt. "Just because I kept my distance didn't mean I forgot about you. You were always part of my world, Matt."

The teenager nodded. Scuffed his toe again. "I, um, the sign says you're hiring."

"We lost one of our baristas the other day. He gave his phone number to some guy's girlfriend and caused a fight."

"Bummer."

"Not really," Chloe chimed in. "Are you looking for a job?"

Matt glanced at her and back to his father with a blush. "I'm going to be spending the summer with friends here in the city, and I thought maybe, I might…"

He was offering an olive branch. Ian, wise man that he was becoming, snatched it. "Let's go inside and I'll tell you about the position."

Chloe lingered on the sidewalk, watching as the man she loved held the door for his son. In a way, she and Ian both had come full circle. After all, if he had never tried to reconnect with his son, the two of them wouldn't have found each other. Without Matt's rejection, Ian never would have learned to forgive himself. Nor would she have learned to take a chance on love. Now, with their lessons learned, Ian might finally have a chance to know his son, as well.

Sometimes you did get what you deserved.

"Hey, Curlilocks," Ian called from the doorway. "Are you coming? I can't do this without you."

And sometime, you got even more.

Her heart fuller than she could imagine, Chloe took Ian's hand and walked inside.

* * * * *

ROMANCE

The Only Woman to Defy Him	Carol Marinelli
Secrets of a Ruthless Tycoon	Cathy Williams
Gambling with the Crown	Lynn Raye Harris
The Forbidden Touch of Sanguardo	Julia James
One Night to Risk it All	Maisey Yates
A Clash with Cannavaro	Elizabeth Power
The Truth About De Campo	Jennifer Hayward
Sheikh's Scandal	Lucy Monroe
Beach Bar Baby	Heidi Rice
Sex, Lies & Her Impossible Boss	Jennifer Rae
Lessons in Rule-Breaking	Christy McKellen
Twelve Hours of Temptation	Shoma Narayanan
Expecting the Prince's Baby	Rebecca Winters
The Millionaire's Homecoming	Cara Colter
The Heir of the Castle	Scarlet Wilson
Swept Away by the Tycoon	Barbara Wallace
Return of Dr Maguire	Judy Campbell
Heatherdale's Shy Nurse	Abigail Gordon

MEDICAL

200 Harley Street: The Proud Italian	Alison Roberts
200 Harley Street: American Surgeon in London	Lynne Marshall
A Mother's Secret	Scarlet Wilson
Saving His Little Miracle	Jennifer Taylor

Mills & Boon® Large Print

May 2014

ROMANCE

The Dimitrakos Proposition	Lynne Graham
His Temporary Mistress	Cathy Williams
A Man Without Mercy	Miranda Lee
The Flaw in His Diamond	Susan Stephens
Forged in the Desert Heat	Maisey Yates
The Tycoon's Delicious Distraction	Maggie Cox
A Deal with Benefits	Susanna Carr
Mr (Not Quite) Perfect	Jessica Hart
English Girl in New York	Scarlet Wilson
The Greek's Tiny Miracle	Rebecca Winters
The Final Falcon Says I Do	Lucy Gordon

HISTORICAL

From Ruin to Riches	Louise Allen
Protected by the Major	Anne Herries
Secrets of a Gentleman Escort	Bronwyn Scott
Unveiling Lady Clare	Carol Townend
A Marriage of Notoriety	Diane Gaston

MEDICAL

Gold Coast Angels: Bundle of Trouble	Fiona Lowe
Gold Coast Angels: How to Resist Temptation	Amy Andrews
Her Firefighter Under the Mistletoe	Scarlet Wilson
Snowbound with Dr Delectable	Susan Carlisle
Her Real Family Christmas	Kate Hardy
Christmas Eve Delivery	Connie Cox

0414 GEN STD LP

Mills & Boon® Hardback
June 2014

ROMANCE

Ravelli's Defiant Bride	Lynne Graham
When Da Silva Breaks the Rules	Abby Green
The Heartbreaker Prince	Kim Lawrence
The Man She Can't Forget	Maggie Cox
A Question of Honour	Kate Walker
What the Greek Can't Resist	Maya Blake
An Heir to Bind Them	Dani Collins
Playboy's Lesson	Melanie Milburne
Don't Tell the Wedding Planner	Aimee Carson
The Best Man for the Job	Lucy King
Falling for Her Rival	Jackie Braun
More than a Fling?	Joss Wood
Becoming the Prince's Wife	Rebecca Winters
Nine Months to Change His Life	Marion Lennox
Taming Her Italian Boss	Fiona Harper
Summer with the Millionaire	Jessica Gilmore
Back in Her Husband's Arms	Susanne Hampton
Wedding at Sunday Creek	Leah Martyn

MEDICAL

200 Harley Street: The Soldier Prince	Kate Hardy
200 Harley Street: The Enigmatic Surgeon	Annie Claydon
A Father for Her Baby	Sue MacKay
The Midwife's Son	Sue MacKay

Mills & Boon® Large Print
June 2014

ROMANCE

A Bargain with the Enemy	Carole Mortimer
A Secret Until Now	Kim Lawrence
Shamed in the Sands	Sharon Kendrick
Seduction Never Lies	Sara Craven
When Falcone's World Stops Turning	Abby Green
Securing the Greek's Legacy	Julia James
An Exquisite Challenge	Jennifer Hayward
Trouble on Her Doorstep	Nina Harrington
Heiress on the Run	Sophie Pembroke
The Summer They Never Forgot	Kandy Shepherd
Daring to Trust the Boss	Susan Meier

HISTORICAL

Portrait of a Scandal	Annie Burrows
Drawn to Lord Ravenscar	Anne Herries
Lady Beneath the Veil	Sarah Mallory
To Tempt a Viking	Michelle Willingham
Mistress Masquerade	Juliet Landon

MEDICAL

From Venice with Love	Alison Roberts
Christmas with Her Ex	Fiona McArthur
After the Christmas Party...	Janice Lynn
Her Mistletoe Wish	Lucy Clark
Date with a Surgeon Prince	Meredith Webber
Once Upon a Christmas Night...	Annie Claydon

Discover more romance at

www.millsandboon.co.uk

- 💜 WIN great prizes in our exclusive competitions
- 💜 BUY new titles before they hit the shops
- 💜 BROWSE new books and REVIEW your favourites
- 💜 SAVE on new books with the Mills & Boon® Bookclub™
- 💜 DISCOVER new authors

PLUS, to chat about your favourite reads, get the latest news and find special offers:

- 🔲 Find us on facebook.com/millsandboon
- 🐦 Follow us on twitter.com/millsandboonuk
- 💜 Sign up to our newsletter at millsandboon.co.uk